HER SECRET BILLIONAIRE ROOMMATE

A CLEAN BILLIONAIRE ROMANCE BOOK SIX

BREE LIVINGSTON

Edited by
CHRISTINA SCHRUNK

Her Secret Billionaire Roommate

Copyright © 2018 by **Bree Livingston**

Edited by Christina Schrunk

https://www.facebook.com/christinaschrunk.editor

Proofread by Krista R. Burdine

https://www.facebook.com/iamgrammaresque

Cover design by Victorine Lieske

http://victorinelieske.com/

Bree Livingston

https://www.breelivingston.com

Her Secret Billionaire Roommate / Bree Livingston. -- 1st ed.

ISBN: 9781793265456

To my family,

Thank you for putting up with my quirks.

CHAPTER 1

*G*abriel Saxon chased two ibuprofens with water and rubbed his left temple with his fingers as his throbbing headache grew. The last thing he needed was to be down with a migraine. Negotiations with Romero Publishing had come to a complete standstill, and he'd just convinced Sylvia Romero to have another meeting with him.

The door to his office opened and his assistant, Albert Mattison, stopped just inside. "Sir, your mother just called. She's on her way up."

Looking up at him, Gabe squinted. The early morning light streaming into his office didn't help him at all. "That's fine," he breathed as his stomach soured.

"Headache?"

He nodded.

"Have you taken anything?"

"Yeah, but not fast enough." Gabe leaned forward with his arms on his desk and buried his face in them. Darkness always helped a little. "Get me some caffeine, will you?"

"Hot or cold?"

He groaned. "I don't care."

"Get him something cold." The smooth lilt of his mother's voice carried from the doorway. "And cancel his appointments for the rest of the day."

Gabe lifted his head. "No, I need to get this deal worked out. Sylvia Romero is flying in. We're finishing this deal today one way or another."

Albert's gaze darted from him to his mother. "Um."

His mother lifted an eyebrow. "Albert, call Mrs. Romero and tell her she'll be meeting with me." She paused, smoothing her knee-length, dark-grey pencil skirt. The slate-blue blouse she wore made her tinsel-silver hair stand out. "After you get my son something cold and caffeinated."

"Yes, ma'am," Albert said and shut the door behind him as he left.

"Mom, we need this deal done. I started it; I need to finish it. Isn't that what you taught me?"

His mother seemed to glide to the chair across from him and sat. "Yes, I did, but I think Mrs. Romero will be more accommodating if speaking to another woman."

Gabe couldn't think. The increased pounding on the left side of his head forced him to bury his face again.

"You should take a break. The doctor told you your stress was causing these headaches. They started right after—"

"Mom." His voice was soft. "Please don't mention her."

Cool fingers wrapped around his hand and squeezed. "Love, you *need* a break. You collapsed two months ago. I didn't push you then because the deal being negotiated at the time depended on you and I know how much you wanted it, but you aren't needed for this deal. You need rest. Your body can't handle any more. You've won, sweetheart. Now it's time to take a moment and recharge."

"I can't."

The door opened, and Albert said, "Here you go."

Gabe looked up as his assistant set a cold soda in front of him. He popped the can open and took a long draw. The drink bubbled in his mouth and felt cool going down.

"I'll call Sylvia Romero now, Mrs. Saxon."

"Thank you, Albert. Would you also make a reservation at the new sushi place that just opened a few blocks away? I've heard nothing but rave reviews, and Mrs. Romero is a sushi lover. Maybe raw fish will get her in a good mood." His mom winked.

Albert grinned. "Yes, ma'am. I'll get right on that." He briskly walked out of the room and shut the door behind him.

"Is it helping?"

The pulsing in his head had lessened, and he took another drink. "A little."

"Good. I've got you packed. You're going to the Snowshoe Creek cabin in Montana."

Gabe looked at his mom. "What?"

"You heard me. You're going to Snowshoe Creek for no less than two weeks. I'm not taking any lip from you either. I've already called ahead, and Denver will have the fridge stocked by the time you get there." Her tone was firm.

"It's January, and it's freezing there."

"Yes, which means you'll have time to relax."

He shook his head and regretted it. With a groan, he laid his head down. "At least send me somewhere warm."

"No. You need this time alone." His mom paused. "Saxon Publishing is stronger than it's ever been, and *when* we buy Romero, we'll be the biggest house in

New York. Your drive has turned us into a billion-dollar company, making you a thirty-year-old billionaire along with it. You don't have to work so hard to be good enough anymore. You've proven yourself."

Had he? *All the money in the world wouldn't make you good enough for me.* It's what she'd said after he'd tracked her down.

"Is she still calling you? Showing up at events she knows you'll be attending?"

Rachelle Yancy. She'd only started coming around again when he made Saxon a name in the publishing world a few months ago. In his head, he knew that was why, but for so long, it had been him and Rachelle. It was hard for his heart to let it go. Every time he saw her, old feelings would surface. "Mom."

His mom stood and walked around the desk to perch on the edge next to him. "Gabriel Alexei Saxon. She's not good for you."

Even with a throbbing left hemisphere, he knew when his mother broke out the three names that she meant business. His sister and two brothers often wondered if their mother had given them three names just so she could wield them like a weapon when she used her scary *don't mess with me* tone.

"I have the jet fueled and ready. As soon as you can get to the car, you're going."

"You seriously packed for me?"

One silver eyebrow went up. "Actually, no, I know how you are, but if you give me any more grief, I will."

"I'll go. I doubt it will do me any good, but I'll go."

The corners of her mouth quirked up. "Good boy."

He'd have rolled his eyes if he thought it wouldn't hurt. "You'll let Albert know?"

"Everything will be taken care of. Believe it or not, I ran this company before you took over, and I can run it again."

Gabe stood and kissed his mother on the cheek. "I'll see you in a couple weeks."

"Or longer if you need it." She cupped his cheek. "Take some time, sweetheart. For me."

He nodded, although he knew no amount of time could fix what was broken by Rachelle. She'd ruined him. But if going to a Montana cabin would put his mom's mind at ease, then he'd do it.

FIRE LICKED the wood in the fireplace as Livy drew her knees to her chest. The laptop sitting next to her was a noose, and every word not written, a stone being thrown. Why couldn't she write? Well, she knew, but in the past when her world fell apart, writing was what helped her rebuild.

Why couldn't she do that now? It had been ten months. Honestly, if she thought hard enough, she could get it down to the number of seconds since catching her fiancé with another woman. Tears pricked her eyes, and she looked up, blinking them back. Was she ever going to stop getting weepy when she thought of Jacob?

A knock on the door drew her attention from the ceiling. Her heart pounded. Who would be knocking on the door? She was five minutes from town in the middle of Snowshoe, Montana. No one but her agent was supposed to know she was even there.

"Who's here?" a man called through the door.

Livy stood and cautiously walked to the door. "Who are you?"

"I asked first."

Her hand trembled as she touched the knob. Did she let him in? Were there serial killers in places like this? "I'm Olivia Weber. I rented this cabin."

"Would you please open the door? It's freezing out here."

What should she do? "I need your name first."

"Gabriel." He paused. "Andrews."

Livy chewed her lip. "How do I know you won't kill me?" May as well be direct.

"Would I have knocked?"

Wasn't Ted Bundy polite?

"Look, I don't want to hurt you. I just want out of this freezing wind."

She hesitated a second and then said, "Fine." She fumbled with the door and opened it. A burst of frosty air hit her cheeks and took her breath away. "Come in."

Stomping his feet on the doormat as he walked in, the man knocked the snow off his shoes and rubbed his hair, flinging snow all over the floor. Without looking at her, he asked, "Why are you here?"

The sharpness of his tone made her jump. "L-like I said, I rented this cabin."

When he lifted his gaze, a burst of electricity coursed through her. Smoldering dark eyes peeking through long lashes held hers. Peeling off his coat revealed a tight long-sleeved shirt that hugged his toned body and showed off every muscle. "I sincerely doubt that. I don't rent this cabin to anyone, so you need to start telling the truth before I call the police and file charges."

Livy blinked. He was perhaps the most gorgeous man she'd ever seen with his tousled dark hair, olive skin, and a clean-shaven face. Holy smokes. It was as though he'd walked out of one of her novels. And he was going to have her arrested.

Her head quickly came back to earth as she shivered at the thought of having her mugshot taken and using a shared toilet. She did not want that experience again. "My friend Tori rented this cabin for me. I don't know where she found it. I swear I have no idea. I didn't even know she'd booked it until she sprang it on me."

Gabriel studied her. "How did you even get in?"

"I got the keys at the diner this afternoon. That's where I was told to get them. Apparently, the owner there takes care of the cabin when no one is staying in it."

He put his hands on his hips. "You can't stay here. I don't know who said you could rent this cabin, but they lied. You need to pack your things and go."

Her heart pounded faster. There was no way to make it to a hotel before dark. She felt the color drain from her face. "I don't know this area. Could I please stay the night and leave in the morning?"

The man took a deep breath, exhaled sharply, and shook his head, seeming annoyed by her mere presence.

"Please? I promise you won't even know I'm here,

and I'll go first thing in the morning."

As he pulled his phone out of his pocket, his gaze landed on her again. "I came up here to get away from people."

Why did she feel so small when he was eyeing her like that? Confidence exuded from him. There was no doubt in her mind he was used to telling people what to do and expecting it to get done.

She fidgeted with her fingers and toed the ground. Her shoulders sagged. "I understand." This man wasn't going to let her stay even if she begged until she was blue in the face. "I'll go pack."

She turned, and he grabbed her elbow. An electrical current raced up her arm, and she jerked her gaze to his. He quickly removed his hand and locked eyes with her.

His features had softened, and those smoldering eyes now looked at her with sympathy. "No, it's fine, but you leave in the morning. Got it?" He paused. "Oh, and I'd like to speak to your friend Tori if you don't mind. Tonight."

Olivia nodded. "Sure, I'll call her right now. I was supposed to FaceTime her when I got here earlier anyway, and I haven't. Air rescue may have been called at this point." She let out a tight laugh.

Why did Tori do this to her?

CHAPTER 2

*L*ivy took a deep breath and grabbed her phone as Gabriel stalked out of the foyer, taking a right and disappearing down the hall.

She heard a door slam and quickly dialed Tori. The phone rang a few times, and her agent appeared on the screen. "It's about time, Livy. When did you get there?"

"Just a couple of hours ago."

Tori grumbled. "And why didn't you call me when you got there like you were supposed to?"

"I don—"

Her friend's eyes widened. "Whoa! Who's the hot guy?"

Livy's skin tingled as Gabriel stopped right behind her. The smell of sandalwood and citrus wafted around her, and it took all her effort not to actually sniff the air. Wow. Did he smell good.

"The hot guy owns the cabin and wants to know who rented it to you," he said gruffly, his breath tickling her neck.

Tori tilted her head. "I got a number through a friend. It was a friend of a friend of a friend kind of thing."

"Do you have their information?"

"Yeah, hold on." Tori set the phone down.

Uncomfortable tension settled around them. It was awkward and awful. If Livy wasn't afraid of the dark so much, she'd go ahead and leave.

Tori reappeared. "Um, a guy named Albert rented it to me."

"Albert?"

"Yeah, Albert Mattison."

"Albert Mattison?"

The tone of his voice made Livy turn around. She stared at him while a look of confusion played on his features. "Do you know him?"

He nodded.

"I got his name from an ag—"

Livy quickly looked back at the phone and tried to discreetly shake her head. This man didn't need to know anything about her. She was only staying the night, and then she was going back home. She hadn't wanted to come anyway.

"You got his name from who?" Gabriel asked.

Tori gave Livy a weird look and shook her head. "I'm an agent in New York, Tori Bennett. This friend of mine, Garland Green, gave it to me." Her friend paused, and her gaze roamed up and down Gabriel's face. "You look very familiar."

Something flashed in Gabriel's eyes, and he waved his hand. "I get told that a lot. And you're an agent?"

"Yes, a literary agent. What's going on?"

Livy chewed her bottom lip. "I don't think the person who rented this cabin to you was in a position to do that. I'm going home tomorrow."

"What? No. I'll find you somewhere else. You need to get that book done."

Squeezing her eyes shut, Livy sighed.

"You're an author?" Gabriel asked as he looked at Livy.

Tori lifted a single eyebrow and smiled. "A b—"

"A brand-new author. I'm not even published yet." The words rushed out of her mouth.

"Right. Well, the person who rented this cabin to you had no right to do so. Ms. Weber will have to find other accommodations tomorrow," Gabriel said.

Livy nodded. "Yes, of course. I will be gone as soon as the sun rises."

"Good."

She held the phone to her chest and dashed to the room she'd taken. At least he wasn't making her move. Peeling the phone away from her, she looked at Tori. "I knew this was a bad idea."

"It's a great idea. Why didn't you tell him you were published?"

"Did you see him?"

Tori grinned. "Oh, I saw him. All six-plus feet of him. Gorgeous, olive skin, and toned. I bet he has abs you could build houses on."

Livy's cheeks heated. "Stop that. This guy thinks I'm horrible. He was coming up here to be alone, and here I am. I wish you hadn't rented this place."

"You needed to get away. This is your last deadline."

She wilted onto the bed and flopped back. "I know. I'm reaching for the words, but they just won't come."

"Honey, your heart was broken, but it's been long enough now. You need to get over Jacob."

The dull ache slowly worked its way back into her soul. "It's not that easy."

"Sure it is. Maybe if you go out there and charm

that dreamy guy, it'll be really easy to get over him." Tori wiggled her eyebrows.

Did Tori not see how he was looking at her? He was not interested in her at all. "Uh, that guy doesn't want anything to do with me. I think if he could, he'd pick me up by my scruff and toss my butt out in the snow."

Tori softened. "Livy, any man who gets the chance to know you, really know you, would never let you go. You're good all the way to your toes. I've never met anyone as forgiving as you."

"Yeah, look what it got me."

"You're only twenty-nine. You've got plenty of time. One day, your Mr. Right will come along, and he'll never even look at another woman."

Livy nodded. "Yeah, you keep saying that. Listen, I'm going to go."

"Okay, but this holiday thing isn't over. You are getting away."

She rolled her eyes. "Whatever. Bye, Tori."

"Bye."

With the call ended, she rolled onto her side and curled into a ball. She didn't want to come here in the first place, and now she had a reason to go home. Tori would have to understand that getting away wasn't going to fix what was wrong with her. There wasn't anything that could fix her.

JERKING AWAKE, Gabe bolted straight up in bed as a loud crash came from somewhere in the house. Then he heard another loud crash. What was going on out there? He looked at his phone. At three in the morning? He threw his covers off and swung his legs over the side of the bed. Storming out of his room, he walked down the hall and stopped at the edge of the kitchen.

The woman who'd fraudulently rented his cabin was standing on a chair in front of an empty cabinet. Food was set out on the counters, and she looked like she was cleaning.

"What are you doing?"

She jumped and screamed, and as she did, her foot slipped.

Without thinking, Gabe rushed forward and caught her before she could hit the floor. Large round eyes stared up at him and then traveled from his face to his bare chest where her palms were pressed flat against it. She looked back up at his face, and a light pink blush covered her cheeks as she pushed her hands against him to be released.

"I can't sleep," she whispered.

Little zaps were racing through him from where her skin touched his. "I can see that," he said and set her down, backing away. His body didn't seem to remember he wasn't interested in finding a woman.

"I-I'm really sorry. I didn't mean to wake you up. My knee hit a can of green beans, and they hit the floor, and then I hit another because it scared me when it fell."

"Can't you count sheep like a normal human being?"

Those big gray eyes stared at him. Gray? It had to be the lighting. "I'll get these put up right now. I won't make another sound." The woman quickly gathered the items off the counter and stuck them back in the cabinets faster than he would have thought possible. "I really am sorry."

She ducked out of the kitchen without another word and walked to the living room. Why wasn't she going to bed?

He followed her to the other room where she sat on the large rug in front of the fireplace. "Why are you staying out here?"

"I can't stay out here even if I'm quiet?" Her voice was soft as she twisted to look at him.

"Why would you want to?"

"I'll just toss and turn in bed. It's nice out here. Maybe the sound of the fire will help me go to sleep."

Gabe parked himself in the chair farthest away from her. "How will you drive home tomorrow if you're so exhausted you can't keep your head up?"

A one-shoulder shrug, and she turned back to the fire. "I have chronic insomnia. I've learned to live with it. I'll get a few hours' sleep, and I'll be fine." She covered her mouth as she yawned again.

He took a deep breath and let it out slowly. Silence stretched out and became uncomfortable. If her story was true, it wasn't her fault she was invading his mother-imposed getaway. He took another deep breath. "Look, I know this wasn't your fault. You just surprised me, and I don't like surprises."

She nodded but stayed quiet.

His knee bounced as silence stretched out again. Why wasn't she talking his head off like every other woman? Finally, when he couldn't take it anymore, he said, "I make a killer hot chocolate. Would you like one? Maybe it'll help you get to sleep."

Slowly, she twisted around. "You'd make me hot chocolate?"

The way she said it made him take another look at her. Her dark hair was pulled up into a messy bun, and the almost too-fluffy bathrobe covered a plain t-shirt and thin dark pajama pants with frogs on them. A little button nose, soft full lips, and cheekbones that were defined but not the slice-you kind made her incredibly attractive. He'd been so flustered when he arrived that he hadn't noticed it before.

"I'm already making one. What's one more?" Gabe stood.

"Thank you." She chewed her thumb. "Um…"

Great. She was going to be one of those women who wanted non-fat almond milk brought down from the peak of the Andes Mountains. "What?"

"Could you put a shirt on?"

He chuckled. "Why? Am I making you nervous?"

She quickly faced the fire. "No, it's fine."

Exhaling sharply, he rolled his eyes as he left her in the living room and walked to his room, slipping on a shirt before coming back into the kitchen. When he said he made a killer hot chocolate, he wasn't thinking he was in a cabin in Montana. He was thinking he was in his penthouse in New York. Hopefully, whoever stocked the kitchen would have thought to include the ingredients for hot chocolate. Other than coffee, what else would a person drink in this type of subzero temperature?

In the third cabinet, he finally found a box filled with packets. He wrinkled his nose. Yuck. He preferred real cocoa, but it would have to do. Once the water was heated, he fixed two cups and took one to the small figure sitting in front of the fire.

He handed her a cup and took a seat about two feet from her. "I hope it's okay. It's not my normal fare. I could only find the boxed stuff."

"I'm sure it's fine. Thank you for making it."

Why did everything that came out of her mouth sound so sad? Maybe a little conversation wouldn't be horrible. He would have nothing but solitude when she was gone. "You said your name is Olivia?"

"Yeah, but most people call me Livy."

"Most people call me Gabe."

She stuck her hand out as she took a sip of her cocoa. "Nice to meet you."

He shook her hand, and again, tiny zaps of electricity shot through him. "You too."

They sat quietly while they drank their hot chocolate and watched the fire die down to a yellow glow. All this quiet was making him antsy. Was this what he could expect when he was all by himself? Would it be wrong to pray for a huge snowstorm so she'd have to stay just so he wouldn't be forced to stay there alone?

"You know, you didn't have to come here just because your agent told you to."

One little shoulder shrugged. "She was just trying to be nice to me. Although, I question her decision to send me to the Arctic Circle."

He chuckled, thinking about his mom. There really had been no choice for him either. "You'd think if people cared, they'd send the people they loved somewhere warm."

A sweet little laugh popped out. It was soft and musical. Something he could listen to on a regular basis. The thought caught him off guard. When was the last time he'd thought that about a woman?

She set her mug down and lay back, covering her mouth as she yawned. "You'd think. I would have preferred Fiji. I mean, don't they have secluded huts there?" She yawned again. "I'm sorry."

He tilted his head and studied her. "Did you sleep at all?"

"No, not really," she whispered.

Looking away, he scrunched his eyebrows together. He'd never met anyone who suffered from insomnia. When he looked in her direction again to ask her about her writing, she'd curled into a ball facing him, and her chest was rising and falling evenly.

Normally, if he were dating her, he'd pick her up and put her in bed, but since he had no idea what she'd think, he covered her with a blanket and took their cups to the sink.

At least she'd be gone tomorrow. He didn't need any house guests, and he certainly didn't need any cute ones that made his heart jump. Olivia Weber needed to go, and quickly.

CHAPTER 3

*W*ith his fingers laced behind his head, Gabe let his mind wander. He stared at the ceiling as early morning sunlight filtered in, and the deafening silence made him dread the coming solitude. He'd avoided being alone because he didn't *want* the chance to think. Now it was all he *could* do.

It was so quiet that his ears rang, making it nearly impossible to sleep, and he'd lain awake most of the night, trying to push thoughts and feelings down that made him hurt all the way to his core.

His chest tightened, and he closed his eyes. Rachelle. He'd loved her with all that was in him, and she'd still left him. What was the point in loving someone when it wasn't enough? Why did his mom think spending weeks alone in a cabin would fix what happened to him? How did you get over not being sufficient for the one person you loved most in the world?

He startled at the sound of luggage wheels rolling down the hall. Sitting up, he rubbed his eyes, tossed his covers off, and stood. The least he could do was see Livy off. She'd be the last person he'd see for a while, and the thought unsettled him. Could he handle this much quiet for two weeks?

He strolled down the hall and out to the living room and then stopped as she came into view. Her shoulder was leaned against one of the windows that lined the back of the house. She'd left her hair down, and it hit the middle of her back in long dark waves. Even from where he stood, the tresses looked silky. She was such a tiny thing, but she sure could fill out a pair of jeans. They hit every bit of her perfectly, and her lavender t-shirt hugged her body as if it had been made just for her.

He was still curious about her writing. Maybe when he satisfied his mom enough that he could go home, he'd call Tori and ask about Ms. Olivia Weber. If she was any good, maybe he'd take a chance on her at Saxon.

Looking past her, pure white snow blanketed everything as far as the eye could see. It was peaceful, and after the last year of continually staying busy, his rat-race mind was having a hard time adjusting. He pictured a straightjacket without having his arms tied.

As Livy turned, she jumped, and her hand went to her throat. "Oh my goodness."

Gabe held his hands up. "I'm sorry. I didn't mean to sneak up on you."

She smiled. "It's okay. I just wanted to take one more look before I left." She paused. "Well, thank you for letting me stay the night. I'll get out of your hair now."

He walked her to the door and said, "I'm sorry your friend was scammed. I'll make sure she gets her money back." He wasn't sure what was going on with Albert. The man had been his father's assistant for years, and he'd stayed on with Gabe. Something had to be wrong for him to do something like this. Once Livy was gone, he was going to find out what. If it were anyone else, they wouldn't be getting a second chance or the benefit of the doubt.

"Thank you. Tori will appreciate that," she said and slipped her coat on. When she opened the door, just beyond the edge of the porch overhang, dark clouds swirled overhead, and her lips parted with a gasp. "Maybe I should check the weather." She shut the door and leaned her back against it.

The thought ran through Gabe's mind as well. Yeah, he wanted her gone, but the clouds filling the sky looked intimidating even to him. He pulled out his phone at the same time she did and tapped his weather app. His gaze flicked between her and his phone.

"I don't think you should leave," he said.

Livy looked up, her gray eyes meeting his. He thought his mind was playing tricks on him the night before, but there they were, holding his gaze and making his pulse jump again. She smiled. "Oh, no, I'm sure it'll be fine. I'm not even supposed to be here. I can make it to town at least, and that way you don't have to put up with me."

"This town is in a valley. If you don't make it to that pass in time and it actually dumps the expected three feet of snow, you'll be stranded. There's no way you'll be able to live in whatever that is parked out there."

"It's a Volkswagen Thing. It's perfectly safe."

He shook his head. "Not in a snowstorm it isn't." He wasn't sure it was safe anywhere. His SUV had barely made it. There was a part of him that wanted to see video of her vehicle actually making it to the cabin.

"Well, what am I supposed to do?" she asked.

He exhaled sharply and pinched the bridge of his nose. So much for spending a couple weeks alone.

"This is a three-bedroom cabin. If we each stay in our corner, we can both get what we came for."

She caught her bottom lip between her teeth and cast her gaze to the floor. "I don't know." When she looked up, his breath caught. Those stunning smoky eyes seemed to bore right through him and rooted him in place. "I mean, I know you don't want me here, and I don't…"

Gabe touched her arm and nearly flinched. The contact sent a bolt of electricity through his body that nearly knocked him to his knees. "There's no way you can beat that storm. I'd feel awful if you got hurt just because I wanted to be alone. I'm sure there will be some snowplows that come through in a few days, and then you can go home. Okay?" He dropped his hand, but it didn't lessen the strange reaction to Livy.

Her gaze darted from him to the door as she hesitated.

Leaving wasn't an option, and he needed to put her mind at ease so she'd stay. "Take your stuff back to your room, and I'll make us some breakfast."

"I don't know. Maybe if I hurry, I can make it out of town. I mean, it doesn't look that close."

He shook his head. "Really, it's okay."

"I'm so sorry. I should have left last night." She straightened and sighed. "Why can't I ever do anything right?" The words were barely audible, and if he hadn't been standing so close, he wouldn't have heard her.

What had she been through to think something like that? But he understood her. Rachelle was never happy with anything he did. "No, it's okay. Really."

With a nod, she wrapped her fingers around her luggage handle and walked down the hall to the last room on the right. While she put her things up, he went to the kitchen to get breakfast started. He hoped it would act as a peace offering, especially since he'd made up the part about the snowplows. There was no telling when they'd arrive. He just hoped the food would hold out until they did.

He glanced over his shoulder as he heard footfalls. "Do you like eggs?"

Livy stopped just inside the kitchen. "I like them scrambled."

"Just scrambled?" He turned and looked at her. That was the only way he liked his too. Rachelle had bugged him to death about trying other ways, but each time he tried them any other way, they turned him green.

"Yeah. I don't eat them any other way."

He smiled. "Okay, scrambled it is." As he searched through the bottom cabinets for a skillet, she took a seat at the bar right in front of the stove. Once he found a pan, he turned the stove on and asked, "So, you're a writer?" He may as well satisfy his curiosity while he cooked.

"Yes."

"And Tori is your agent?" He cracked eggs into the pan as he glanced at her.

Livy nodded. "Yeah, she's as much my friend as my agent."

"How long have you known her?"

"About eight years."

He finished with the egg carton and put it away before tossing the shells. Returning to the stove, he asked, "Is that how long you've been trying to get published?"

Her eyes widened. "Um, no."

Something about the way she said it piqued his curiosity. "Did you know her before she became an agent?"

Livy groaned. "No."

Heat traveled up his neck. He hated being lied to. The last few months with Rachelle had been nothing but lies. "Okay, look, I hate being lied to. If you're going to stay here, I should at least know who I'm rooming with."

"I'm not trying to lie. I actually hate lying, but…"

"Why don't you just shoot straight with me?"

Her shoulders sagged. "You're right." She chewed her thumb. "If I tell you, you have to promise to never tell anyone. I have a pen name for a reason."

"Okay, what?" It came out a little harsher than he intended.

"I'm published under the name of Amelia Hurst. You've probably never even heard of me because I'm a romance author."

Amelia Hurst? It took a level of control he didn't know he had to not let the shock show on his face. She was the jewel of Romero Publishing, and if he remembered correctly, she owed them a book. It was over a year late. He'd verify it, but he rarely forgot things like that. Did he tell her he knew? He'd given her his mother's maiden name as a false last name, and he knew nothing about her. What if she found out and tried to use him like Rachelle?

"You're right. I don't think I've heard of that name." He wondered if she knew who he was. It wasn't like he wasn't known in the publishing world.

With Gabe's leadership, Saxon had made a huge splash in the world of publishing right after his father died. They'd signed a book deal with H. F. Easterly, and his young adult series had changed the face of the genre. It was Gabe's gut that propelled him to sign the unknown author, but he had been certain the planned series would be a hit, and it was.

"Who's your publisher?"

"Romero Publishing."

Gabe nodded and turned the eggs. "I think I've heard of them."

CHAPTER 4

*L*ivy smiled. "You have?"

"My ex-girlfriend was a romance reader."
He looked at her as he scrambled the eggs. "I'm pretty sure that was the publisher." There was a forcefulness in the way he said ex-girlfriend. She wished she could be strong when it came to Jacob.

What would he think if she told him her next book was a year overdue? Why would she tell him that? She didn't know him. "I like them. They've treated me well."

"Do you sell a lot of books?" He seemed genuinely interested, which was a first for her. Most men didn't care at all, especially Jacob. Even with six figures coming in, it was her little writing hobby. He'd even made fun of her when he'd tried to read a few of her novels.

She nodded and felt heat rush to her cheeks. It was embarrassing to tell people she was successful. She wasn't sure why. "Actually, I'm a New York Times Bestselling Author for the last seven years running."

Gabe stopped mid-stir and stared at her. "Really? Do you have a new book out now?"

Why did he have to ask that question? The only reason she told him about her pen name was that she didn't like lying or hiding things from people. She was all too familiar with the hurt it caused. "No. That's why I'm here. I…I've had trouble writing, and my next deadline is soon. I can't miss another one."

With the eggs finished, he dished them out and slid a plate in front of her. Then he took a seat two stools over. As she took a bite, he asked, "Why have you had so much trouble?"

She stuffed the eggs into her mouth to give herself a minute to think. There was no shortcut to that answer. Tears threatened to spill, and she looked away. "I don't know you very well, and I really don't want to answer that."

"Okay." His voice was soft, and it almost felt as though he understood. "Do you have any ideas about the new book?"

"No," she said softly and looked at him. The conversation needed to change direction. "How about you? What do you do?"

Gabe finished chewing the bite in his mouth before answering. "I'm in acquisitions with a company in New York City."

"What do you typically acquire?"

"Mostly paper-related things, like books."

Antique books? "That sounds interesting." She covered her mouth as she yawned. Her late night was creeping up on her, and along with a full stomach, it was making her sleepy.

"If I didn't know about your midnight cleaning rampage, I'd wonder about your sincerity." He chuckled.

Heat warmed her cheeks. "I'm really sorry for waking you up last night."

"Honestly, I was having trouble sleeping anyway. All this quiet has me a little out of sorts."

Livy finished her eggs, slipped off the stool, and walked to the sink. "I've had trouble sleeping since I was young." With her back to Gabe, she leaned against the counter and washed the plate.

"Where are you from?"

She glanced over her shoulder. "Orlando. I've spent most of my life in Florida."

"Most?"

Another piece of her she didn't want to explain to a stranger. Something for someone to feel sorry for her about. She might be pathetic, but that didn't mean she wanted someone's pity. "I moved around a lot." More like she moved families. "How about you?"

"Born and raised in New York City."

"Do you like it there?" She finished washing her dish and dried it.

Gabe shrugged. "Yeah, I do, but sometimes I wonder if it would be nice to live somewhere with a slower pace."

She'd gone to see Tori, but it had only been short visits. "I've been there a couple of times, so I think I understand that," she said as she put the plate back in the cabinet. "Thank you for breakfast. I think I'll go find my corner of the cabin." She needed to call Tori and let her know what was going on anyway.

"Oh, sure. I was just about to do the same thing."

Livy nodded and walked to her room, shutting the door behind her. Grabbing her phone off the nightstand, she plopped onto the bed and stretched out as she dialed her friend.

"Are you headed home?" Tori asked.

"Well, hello to you too, and no, I'm not."

She chuckled. "Decided to take my advice, eh?"

Closing her eyes, she sighed. "No, there's a snow-storm that's supposed to dump three feet of snow. I can't make it out before it is supposed to get here, so I'm stuck until snowplows arrive in the next few days."

"Don't tell me you're going to stay in your room the whole time and not talk to him."

What could she say? The last time he'd touched her, she'd nearly melted through the floor. His eyes were some of the most intense she'd ever looked into. And that tousled hair? It was all she could do not to run her fingers through it. To say he was good-looking was an understatement.

Livy rolled to her side and switched the phone to her other ear. "No, but he said we should each stay in our own corner. I'm not even supposed to be here, and he wants to be alone. It would be rude to not try to give him the space he wants."

"He sure is hot, though. I'm not sure I could resist being all up in his space."

A small giggle bubbled out. "That's not funny."

"Admit it. You think he's gorgeous."

"No. I mean, yes, but stop it."

"You think he's gorgeous. You want to date him. Love him and—"

Livy rolled her eyes and laughed. "Shut up, Sandra."

Tori barked with laughter. "I can't help it if *Miss*

Congeniality is the best movie ever made and that I've got it memorized. Some people just have zero taste."

Over the course of eight years, their relationship had moved from writer and agent to friends. Tori was the only one willing to put up with her quirks. Oh, she'd met people, even had friends, but she was too easygoing, and most of the friends she made ended up being so-called friends.

"You should have come with me," Livy said.

"I'm glad I didn't. Rumor is going around that Romero is being bought by Saxon."

Livy bolted straight up. "What?"

"It's just a rumor, but if that's true, you need to get that book turned in. No way will Saxon keep you. I've got two clients with them. When they give you a deadline, you meet it or you don't have a contract anymore."

It felt as though the world was crashing in around her. How was she supposed to write a romance when her heart was broken? "I'll get it written." She shoved as much confidence into the statement as she could muster.

"That's my girl. Forget about that Jacob jerk. There is love out there for you, Liv. Someone who will soak up all the good things about you and make your weaknesses not so weak."

A tear trickled down her cheek, and she swiped at it. "Yeah, I know."

"Oh, hey, I need to go. Call me later, okay? Tell me how the book's coming."

Livy nodded. "You bet."

They said their goodbyes, and she ended the call. Her heart was in her shoes. Tori would be expecting chapters from her, and she didn't know if she had them in her.

Liv dropped back onto the bed. Maybe she'd luck out and that snowstorm would pass by them. Luck. Yeah right. She could chug a juiced leprechaun and she'd still come up short in the luck department.

As soon as Livy heard Gabe's bedroom door shut that night, she gathered up her blankets, quietly opened her door, and tiptoed to the living room. Through the day, she'd successfully stayed in her corner of the cabin, even when he offered to cook her dinner, which was nice, but he'd been so adamant about being alone that she didn't want to take that away from him.

Being polite was something she understood, and in her mind, the way to return his kindness was to stay in her room as much as possible. She understood all too well wanting some space and no one listening. Plus, she was a complete stranger. Who wants to spend time cooped up in a cabin with someone they don't even know?

The fire had gone out, and now the wall of windows Livy loved made the place an ice den. Snow piles from the promised storm didn't curb the frosty feeling either. Shivering, she hugged herself and rubbed her arms. At least there was still some firewood sitting next to the fireplace so she didn't have to brave the cold to get more.

Once she had the blankets spread out and the logs placed, she turned on the gas and struck a match to get a new fire going before turning the gas off again. She'd never been more thankful for her limited experience with fireplaces in her life. Kneeling in front of it, she held her hands out.

Closing her eyes, she took a deep breath and let the warmth fill her. She loved how the smell reminded her of the last Christmas she had with her parents. It always made her a little sad, but she was glad the memory was still vivid.

"What are you doing?"

Livy squeaked and fell sideways. "Oh my goodness! Are you some kind of ninja, or are you determined to give me a heart attack?"

Gabe threw his head back and laughed. "I'm sorry. I swear I'm not trying to scare you."

"It's not that funny."

"You fell over. That was funny."

She lifted herself onto her knees again and glanced at him. "Okay, maybe it was a little funny."

He wandered over and sat on the floor next to her.

His nearness made her heart race. All she'd have to do is reach out, and her fingers could glide through his hair. What was her thing with hair? Not to mention those sultry dark eyes of his. When he looked at her, it felt like she was a story and he was trying to pull the words off her page.

Livy quickly glanced at him. "I'm sorry if I woke you up or bothered you."

"But you couldn't sleep?"

Shaking her head, she forced herself to keep her gaze on the fire instead of his face. "No."

"May I ask why?"

How could she answer that? She didn't really talk about that stuff with anyone. Then again, Tori was always telling her she needed a therapist. Once she left the cabin, she'd never see him again. Although, he did know her pen name now, but he was a guy. Did guys remember the names of romance authors?

"It's okay if you don't want to tell me." It sounded as though there was sadness in his voice.

Livy quickly glanced at him again, and there he was, staring at her. There was something besides the sultry look too. Instead of shying away this time, she held his gaze. The tension in her shoulders seemed to ebb away. "It's just...I don't...I've never really told anyone before." Well, except for Tori, but that was different.

He continued his intense stare. "I'm an excellent secret keeper."

"I worry. All the time." That was the simplest answer. Telling him she had nightmares would lead to questions she didn't want to answer.

His head tilted, and one eyebrow went up. "Worry?"

Of course, he wasn't any different. Most people didn't understand that it wasn't as simple as *let it go* or *just don't worry.* Why did she say anything? She pulled her gaze from his, and disappointment settled in her stomach. "Never mind." If someone couldn't stick with her beyond that, she didn't see the point in continuing. It's why she never spoke of it.

"No, I'm listening. I won't say anything else until you're done. Please continue."

She looked at him. He seemed genuinely interested. At least he didn't laugh. That's what most people did. Either that or tried to give her advice. "My parents died when I was eight, and there wasn't any family that wanted us."

"Us?"

"Me and my twin baby sisters." Her gaze dipped to the floor.

"I'm so sorry," he whispered.

Livy lifted her head and looked at him. His condolence actually sounded sincere. "It's okay."

"What happened?" he asked as he drew one leg up and stretched the other out.

Her stomach twisted as she thought about her siblings. She only knew a little about her twin sisters. Neither of them wanted her. "We were split up and put into foster homes. My two baby sisters got to stay together and were eventually adopted."

"And you?"

"I was bounced around quite a bit, and after the second time, I started wondering if it was me. By the time I'd been placed with my fifth family, I was having trouble sleeping because I'd lay in bed worrying if I was going to be sleeping in the same bed the next night." She'd keep the darkest part to herself. No one needed to know that.

His hand covered hers, and it felt so small in his. "I

think I'd have trouble sleeping too. It's never gotten better?"

Jacob. "A few years ago it did, and then it's gotten worse again over the last couple of years. Worse than it was before."

He pulled his hand away and draped it over his knee. "Have you tried taking medication?"

She snorted. "Yes."

A smile played on his lips. "There's a story there, huh?"

"It just didn't work well. I was either so groggy I couldn't stand up straight or wired. So wired that a cop pulled me over because my behavior was suspicious, and he took me to jail to have me tested for drugs."

His eyes widened. "No way."

She looked at him and chuckled. "It was so embarrassing. I stopped taking anything."

"And you still worry now that you're older?"

She tangled her fingers in the hem of her shirt and twisted it. "I...After you haven't been wanted for a while, you start to think that no one wants you. You analyze every interaction you have. Was the person being honest? Were they just being nice? It spirals from there. I have a hard time shutting my mind down."

His fingertips slid across her forearm. Tingles followed in their wake, but he was just being sympathetic. "Don't do that. I don't know you well at all, but from the little I'm seeing, you have nothing to worry about."

A compliment? Really? For her?

He seemed to study her as his gaze roamed over her face. "Are you tired?"

CHAPTER 5

*N*ow that Gabe was really looking at Livy, her eyes had deep, dark circles around them.

"I'm…" She swallowed hard, and it looked as though she was trying to decide what to say. "Yeah, all the time."

"How do you write when you're tired like that?"

She chewed her bottom lip. "It wasn't this bad when I started. The past couple of years have been the worst."

If it was confession time, he may as well be honest too. "I get migraines."

"Oh, those are awful."

He lifted his eyebrows. If she had migraines on top of her insomnia, it was a miracle she was able to function at all. "Do you get migraines too? Wouldn't surprise me if you do."

"No, but one of my foster moms got them. She'd have to go lie down in the dark, and sometimes it took hours for them to go away. They'd have her in tears. I was gone before I knew why she got them."

He took a deep breath. "Mine are a product of stress." They'd started right after he'd split with Rachelle.

"I guess a company depending on you to acquire things would be stressful. I can see the need for getting away." She palmed her forehead. "And here I am, gumming it up."

"Actually, I know I said we could find our own corners, but the quiet is killing me. Is there any chance our corners could be a little closer?"

A bubbly laugh escaped, and she pressed her fingers to her lips. He'd liked it the night before, and he wanted to hear more of it. Her lips spread into a smile. "I guess. I was only trying to do what you asked."

"I know, and I'm sorry I was so gruff."

Her hand touched his, and his stomach did a flip as tingles traveled through his hand and up his arm. "No, you had every right to be upset. I understand." She smiled and pulled her hand away.

"So, what do you say? Maybe we have meals together and talk in the evening. Maybe that'll be a good balance."

Worry lines creased her forehead, and she chewed her thumb. "Are you sure? You don't have to be nice because of what I told you. I can stay out of your way so I don't bother you."

"I'm positive, and it doesn't have anything to do with what you shared. I'm used to New York City, and I'm peaced out. I'm ready for some company."

Another bubbly laugh popped out. "Okay." Geez, she had an incredible laugh.

After everything she'd been through, it was no wonder she struggled with self-worth and feeling like a burden to everyone she was around. He hadn't helped her complex any with the way he'd treated her the night before. He'd have to make it up to her somehow.

He wanted to learn more about her, but with what she'd already shared, he'd be pushing his luck. When he'd asked her about her insomnia, he'd never expected her to be so open. Everyone he knew was guarded and closed off.

"What made you start writing?" he asked. That was a safe question she was probably used to answering.

Her full pink lips spread into a cute smile. That was

twice that the word had popped into his head. Mentally, he took out his red pen and slashed through cute. She was an attractive woman, yes, but that didn't mean he had to be attracted *to* her. She was only there until the snowplows arrived, and he'd be calling about them in the morning.

"Oh, I started writing when I was in middle school. It gave me a way to escape."

Gabe leaned back on his elbows. "Why did you pick romance?"

Livy stretched out and laid her hands over her stomach. "I wanted to be loved, and I figured if I couldn't be loved, then I could create someone and give it to them."

"I think I might have to get one of your novels and read it, then."

She laughed as she rolled her head to look at him, and then she quickly looked away. "No, don't do that." The words were barely above a whisper.

"Why? I bet they're great. Can't a guy read romance?"

A soft sigh escaped her lips. "They can, but I'm sure there are better out there."

The sadness in her voice made him look at her. "Why would you say that?"

She waved him off. "I'm just tired. I haven't slept since I woke up last night."

He rolled onto his side and faced her. "When did you wake up?"

"I'm not really sure. I just know it was still dark."

His jaw dropped. "You were worried about being here. I'm so sorry."

She shrugged as she looked at him and said, "Not your fault." Her eyelids looked so heavy that he hurt for her.

"You have my word that I'm happy to have you here. I couldn't make it an entire day being alone. I think I would have gone insane if you weren't here."

Livy smiled as she rolled to face him, tucking her hands under her head. "I think the person who built this cabin was an evil mastermind."

Gabe chuckled. "Oh yeah?"

Her eyes closed, and she nodded. "Mmmmhmmm. You can't get away from it all when what you're trying to get away from is in your head and heart."

Man, did she ever have that right. He was looking in a mirror when he looked at her. Without thinking, he closed the distance between them until he was inches from her. "If you fall asleep, do you want me to put you in bed? I was afraid to last night."

"There's no point. I'll just wake up."

Before he could stop himself, he pushed her hair back from her face. It was as satiny as he imagined.

A soft moan came from her throat, and her body relaxed.

He slipped his fingers through her hair again.

"You smell nice," she whispered.

The sound of her voice made him freeze, and she whimpered. How could anyone not want her? From what he'd seen, she was the human version of cotton candy. Her laugh was great. She had the most incredible eyes. Why did people have to be so cruel?

She took a long, deep breath and let it out slowly. This time he knew she was asleep.

His head screamed for him to get up and go to his room, while his heart kept him rooted in place. Would it really hurt to stay close to her and let her sleep? Gabe swallowed hard. This had the potential to get really sticky for him. She was likable. They were stuck together. Maybe he should have kept their original deal.

He'd stay with her this one night, and he wouldn't stay long. Just an hour or two. Then he'd go, and while he wanted their corners to be closer, this was getting too close.

Gabe didn't mind her staying, but whatever these feelings were that she was awakening in him needed to stay dormant. His heart was off-limits. Friendship was as close as he was willing to get.

THE SMELL of bacon and eggs drifted past Livy's nose, and she opened her eyes. She sat up and rubbed her face with her hands. To the right, through the wall of windows, she could see that the snowstorm had more than delivered its promise of snow, and it was still falling as heavy as an Amazon rainstorm.

"How are you feeling?" Gabe asked.

She jumped and then turned, smiling. "I'm okay." Pushing off the floor, she stood and walked to the bar, taking a seat at the same stool she had the day before.

"Want some breakfast?"

Her stomach grumbled loudly, and her cheeks burned. "Apparently, I do."

He shot her a smile that made her thankful she was already sitting down. "It's almost done."

"I guess that snowstorm is still going, huh?"

"Yeah, last I checked, it slowed down, and the predicted three feet has gone up a couple. Which also means the snowplows are going to be delayed too."

Livy chewed her bottom lip, and she groaned. If she'd just gone home that night instead of being a wimp, she wouldn't be bothering him, even if he did say he liked her being around. He was thinking a couple of days, not who knows how long.

"Hey," he said, and she looked at him. "It's okay."

Could she really be that easy to read? Based on her one and only trip to Vegas, that was a resounding yes. Hanging her head, she squeezed her eyes shut. How was she ever going to sleep again? What if he wasn't being truthful? What if he was just being nice? No one wanted her. Sure, they wanted her stories, her money, her time...but her? Just her? She was useless, and now he was pitying her.

Her chair twisted, and Gabe hooked a finger under her chin. "Look at me," he said.

She slowly opened her eyes, and her lips parted with a soft gasp. His face was inches from hers, and he was looking at her with those intense dark eyes.

"It's okay. I mean it. I'd never tell you that if it wasn't true."

Never was a long time, and in her experience, it only lasted long enough for people to get what they wanted from her.

He kept his dark eyes trained on her, seeming to will her to believe him. Had he been used like that too?

"I promise," he said, and the conviction in his tone made her pause.

Her heart skipped a few beats, and her mouth was dry. Usually, she'd press forward *wanting* to trust people, but for some reason, something about Gabe felt different. She didn't just *want* to trust him. For some crazy reason, she *did* trust him. "Okay."

Silence stretched as he held her gaze, and her heart raced ever faster, causing the blood to rush in her ears. What was going on with her? Oh, right, he was touching her. Tingles were zipping through her from where his finger lingered on her chin. Goosebumps traveled down her spine, and she nearly wiggled in her seat.

His Adam's apple bobbed, and he dropped his hand as he stepped back. "Good. Breakfast is ready."

Their conversation during breakfast was light, and once breakfast was finished, Livy washed dishes while Gabe sat at the bar. She liked this arrangement. He cooked; she cleaned.

"Are you working on a new book? Is that why your agent booked this cabin for you?" he asked.

Her shoulders sagged. "Yeah."

"How's it coming?"

She turned and faced him. He was staring straight at her, and, boy, was he something. If she wasn't leaned against the counter, she was sure she'd be a puddle on the floor. How could anyone be that good-looking? "It's not. I can't get past the first paragraph."

His eyebrows furrowed. "Why?"

Explaining that was something she just couldn't do. "Um, I can't get it to flow." That wasn't a total lie.

He smiled. "Don't authors outline?"

"Some do, but I don't. Well, I kinda do. I write out a sentence for each chapter, but for the most part, I wing it."

"Oh. How does that work?"

She laughed and turned back to the sink. "It's called pantsing. Like writing by the seat of your pants. Usually it works for me."

"But not now?"

"I've got the outline done, but I just can't get the words out."

"Oh."

Livy finished washing the dishes and hung the towel over the faucet. "Well, I think I'm going to go try to write. See you later?"

He nodded. "Sure." The way he said it, she could have sworn he sounded disappointed. That couldn't be right, though.

She left the kitchen and slipped behind the door of her room, leaning against it. Gabriel Andrews was checking all her boxes and then some. Her jets needed to find some ice water and cool down.

Her heart wasn't ready for that, and he was out of her league anyway. She was twenty pounds overweight, no matter what her doctor said. There was no way she could compete with sophisticated New York City women. When she'd visited, every woman she'd seen had been so put together and beautiful.

She pushed off the door and shoved away the crazy thoughts. In a few days, she'd be leaving. She could keep it together that long. Hopefully.

CHAPTER 6

Staring up at the ceiling, Gabe groaned. After breakfast, Livy had washed the dishes and disappeared into her room. He had said he wanted meals together and then they could talk in the evening. Why couldn't he have said something else? Once she'd gone to her room, the emptiness of the cabin started closing in on him, and he'd retreated to his room too.

He rubbed his face with his hand. The night before, he was wanting to go back to keeping their distance, but he was drawn to her. He'd hooked his finger under her chin, and her little lips had been so close and looked so soft. His heart had hammered in his chest to the point that it was painful.

For the past hour, he'd been working out—

pushups, sit-ups, things he could do in his room—
while fighting himself to keep from thinking about
her. He'd been so close to Olivia that he could almost
taste her bubblegum-colored lips. He bet they were
just as soft as her hair. It only made him wonder if
they actually tasted like bubblegum.

He groaned again and rolled onto his side. What
was he thinking, getting that close? Then he remembered. He didn't want her to spend another night
worrying because of him. It was the only thing he
could think of to make sure she heard him.

From there, his thoughts drifted to waking up with
her next to him. The night before, he'd fallen asleep
watching her, and when he woke up, he found himself
with his arm draped over her waist and her back tight
against him. What bothered him most wasn't that
they'd ended up like that. What bothered him was how
great it felt to have her body molded against his.

There was something so comfortable about her.
The way her eyes would hold his and the gentleness in
the way she spoke, and she was so open. Plus, she was
just beautiful. It was hard not to simply sit and stare at
her. She didn't know it either. Of that, he was certain.

He needed to call his mom and tell her what
happened, but he wasn't sure yet if he wanted to give
Albert a raise or press charges. Being confined to the

cabin by himself would have been torture, and now he was sharing it with a beautiful sweet woman. All because his assistant had rented out his cabin without his knowledge.

His phone rang, and he grabbed it off the night-stand. "Hey, Mom," he said as he answered it and put it to his ear. How weird that she was calling him right as he was thinking about her.

"Hey, love. I thought you'd want to know that Romero Publishing is now ours."

Gabe sat up straight and smiled. "You did it?"

"This old woman's still got it."

Psh. "You are not old. Tell me what happened."

"Well, Sylvia does enjoy her sushi, and the new place I booked had her cooing like a baby. We worked out a deal to keep her authors for the next five years. She wanted to take care of them, and I agreed."

He collapsed back on the bed. "Good call. I definitely wanted to be there. She must not have liked me."

"Oh, no, love, she adored you. She was just playing hardball. Our lawyers are hashing out the details, and the deal should be ready for your signature when you get home."

"Once the deal is signed, we'll make the announcement."

"That's what I said too. I promised to take heads if

anything leaked." She paused. "So, enough about work. How is it at the cabin?"

He touched his hand to his forehead. Should he tell her? He switched the phone to his other ear. What was the point in keeping it from her? She knew Albert as well as he did. "Albert has been renting this cabin out without our knowledge."

"What?" Her voice went up two octaves. "Was someone there?"

"Uh, yeah, and they kinda haven't left."

She sucked in a sharp breath. "What?"

"You'll never believe who it is either."

"Who?"

"Olivia Weber. Also known as Amelia—"

"Amelia Hurst?" The name came out just above a whisper.

His eyebrows knitted together. "Yeah. How'd you know that?"

"Are you kidding? She's *the* best romance author out there. I've read everything she's written. They're so full of heart and soul. I haven't gotten through a single one without crying." Another sharp gasp. "Have you told her about the deal?"

"No, she doesn't even know who I am."

"She's an author. She knows who you are."

He squeezed his eyes shut. "I might have told her my last name was Andrews."

"You used my maiden name? Why?"

"I got here, and there was a car out front. I had no idea who was on the other side of the door. I wasn't going to give them my real name."

"Okay, I understand that, but have you come clean yet?"

"No, I don't know how, and it's kinda nice being a regular guy."

He could almost see his mom's face. The one where one of her perfectly trimmed eyebrows arched up and her lips were spread in a smile, like she could read his thoughts. "Oh really?"

"It's not like that, and she's only here until this snowstorm is gone. Which reminds me, I need to call about the snowplows and when we should expect them."

"I see." She took a deep breath. The kind that said, *I want to talk more about this, but I know you'll just be evasive, so I'm changing the subject now.* She waited a breath and said, "So, Albert."

Man, was Gabe glad she wasn't pressing him about Livy, even though he knew that once she did, it would be even worse.

"Has he mentioned anything to you about his family?" he asked. "My gut says something's going on. He would never do this if there wasn't."

"No, I've heard nothing."

"Well, before you take his head, maybe ask. He's been loyal to us, and there has to be a reasonable explanation. If he needs money, we'll give it to him."

"Love, you are so much like your dad. You have the best heart."

He knew where she was going.

She continued. "What Rachelle did to you was beyond low. You deserved better."

"I don't want to talk about it." He couldn't keep the ache out of his voice.

"I love you, Gabe. I'll see you in a week and a half."

"I love you too."

The call ended, and he tossed the phone onto the bed next to him.

Olivia Weber had trusted him with her secrets. What if his vault got a little spring cleaning? Would she keep his secrets like he'd keep hers? Every time he tried to talk about Rachelle, he got sick to his stomach. She'd left him at the altar, but that wasn't the worst thing she'd done. No one knew about that. He wasn't sure he'd ever be able to push the words out.

Livy was easy to be around. A sweetness exuded from her. And after all she'd been through, she had this…peace about her. Not a resigned type of peace, but the kind of peace that allowed her to look at the world without jaded eyes.

Gabe rubbed his face with his hands. What was he even thinking? He didn't know this woman. His secrets were his, and they were going to stay that way.

JERKING AWAKE, Gabe sat up. He was sure he heard Livy's door. His hand froze as he grabbed a handful of his covers to throw off. So what if she got up in the middle of the night? That wasn't his problem. He flopped back down and rolled onto his side, putting his back to the door. Like that would actually make a difference.

All day long he'd been running out of his room the moment he heard her door open like it was a lunch bell ringing and he was starving to death. He'd been the one wanting corners, and now he was desperate for contact.

He sat up and raked a hand through his hair. Nope. He wasn't going out there. Not this time. This time she was on her own.

His bare feet hit the floor with a splat like there was a disconnect with his brain. What if she was having trouble sleeping? With the way her eyes looked, she wasn't lying when she said she had chronic insomnia.

His knees bounced, and he white-knuckled the edge of the bed. With a frustrated sigh, he stood up and nearly tripped over himself as he exited his room. It was too stinking quiet and dark. Out in the middle of nowhere, it was a black hole, and he needed some light.

Livy turned as he entered the living room, like she expected him. "I woke you up when I dropped the log, didn't I?"

"No. I didn't even hear it."

She turned the gas on in the fireplace, struck a match, and it roared to life. The heat radiating from the fire took the bite out of the chill in the living room. As she shut off the gas and turned to him, she hugged herself. "Are you okay? You keep waking up in the middle of the night."

His heart fluttered as her big pewter eyes locked with his. Speaking was out of the question, so he just nodded.

"I could make you some hot chocolate if you want." Her lips spread into a smile that had his heart pounding so hard he was nearly deaf.

He smiled in response. His whole body had gone

insane. What was wrong with him? He needed to get a grip. She knew nothing about him, and he knew almost nothing about her. Except, he did know about her childhood, and from the way she'd looked at him, it wasn't something she talked about often. "You have any qualifications to make hot chocolate? 'Cause that's serious business where I'm from."

Her light bubbly laugh was a siren's call. "I'm sorry, no, but with it being from a box, I think I can manage. I'm an excellent reader."

Gabe nodded and laughed. It had been a long time since he felt so relaxed with someone. "Well, then, don't let me stop you." He waved his hand toward the kitchen.

"Okay," she said as she walked past him. "Take a seat."

He slipped onto a stool in the kitchen as she pulled down the box of hot chocolate and took out two envelopes. Then she filled the tea kettle with water, set it on the stove, and turned the burner on.

She chewed her lips a minute and then smiled when her gaze caught his. "I do have a confession to make."

"Oh yeah?"

"I once burned pasta."

He laughed. "Really?"

Livy nodded. "Yep. I put it on the stove to boil, and I got so involved with a story that I forgot it. All of a sudden, there was all this smoke, and I ran into the kitchen."

"Oh man."

"The pasta was black, and the pan was toast."

"Did it ruin the stove?"

She shook her head. "No, this was before being signed with Tori. I had this old electric stove with burners."

He leaned forward with his arms on the bar. Man, she was gorgeous. Beyond gorgeous. She had a goodness that seemed to radiate off of her. Her beauty came from a depth he'd never experienced before. "I would love to have seen that."

"Yeah, but the smell was awful. It took me two days to air out that stink."

He wrinkled his nose. "I bet."

The kettle squealed, and she turned off the burner as she slid the kettle off. She found two mugs, dumped the contents of the packets in, and then poured the water over them. Grabbing a couple of spoons, she stirred his first and gave it to him and then finished hers.

"I think I'm going to wait to even try this because I don't want to scorch my mouth," she said.

"Want to drink these by the fire?"

"Isn't that the only place to drink them?" Her lips curved up as she caught her bottom lip in her teeth.

Just when he thought his heart would slow down, she did that, and off it sped again. He stood and followed her back to the living room, joining her a few feet from the fire as she sat on the floor. Rachelle would have never been satisfied with this. It was too mundane for her, even if it meant they got time alone.

If he'd just picked up on the clues sooner, maybe he'd have spared himself some heartache. She didn't want him. She wanted his lifestyle. The rubbing elbows with New York elite, parties, and her picture on the front of the latest social magazine. She wanted to climb the social ladder, and that was it.

Warm fingers curled around his hand, and he looked at her.

"I'm sorry you're hurting."

He jerked his hand away. "You don't know anything."

Her lips parted as she nodded. "Okay." Turning back to the fire, she put distance between them.

Why did he do that? She was only being sweet, and he'd bitten her head off. "I'm sorry. I'm so used to…"

"It's okay," she said softly. "I understand. People want you to pour your heart out to them like somehow talking about it will help, but they don't get it. They think things can be fixed, but sometimes something's so broken you can't find all the pieces."

Gabe couldn't catch his breath. Someone finally understood. He wasn't being pestered to *get it out*. As though somehow that would magically fix everything that went wrong.

Livy moved closer again. "Sometimes what you need is for someone to just sit next to you and let you hurt."

Without a word, he took a sip of his drink. He didn't know what to say to her. There was a part of him that wanted to put his arm around her as they sat in front of the fire, and the other part wanted to run as fast and as far away as possible. Livy Weber was different, and it was quickly becoming evident that they shared more than he cared to admit.

CHAPTER 7

or the third day in a row, Livy's field of vision outside the window was filled with dark clouds. Maybe it was the universe's way of patting her on the back and saying, "There, there. I understand." She'd returned to her room after she finished her hot chocolate the night before. There was no sleeping, but she'd chosen to stay in her room.

She curled her arm under her head and let the world around her blur while her thoughts rolled in like the clouds outside. Gabe had snapped at her, but she understood. More than he knew. The kind of hurt she felt coming from him was something she'd experienced more times than she could count.

So far, writing had been useless. She'd started the first paragraph sixty different ways, and none of them were good. Her sorrow seemed to keep seeping from her fingers onto the keyboard. How could she give her characters something she wanted so bad? When would it be her turn to be loved and wanted? Her world of happily ever afters wasn't enough anymore.

It had been an escape in the beginning, but now it was just a world she didn't belong in anymore. Her characters had the life she wanted, and they were mocking her.

A small knock came from the door, and she sat up. Maybe if she didn't say anything, he'd be able to get the space he'd come for.

"Livy. I...I was wondering if you would have lunch with me. Please."

She chewed her thumb as her stomach grumbled.

"I'm going a little insane with all the quiet."

Pushing her covers off, she slipped off the bed, went to the door, and opened it. A big smile greeted her, and if she wasn't mistaken, he sighed in relief.

"Lifesaver."

Her heart pounded. *Lifesaver?* Her? "What's for lunch?"

"There's a ton of cold cuts and some tomatoes and lettuce. I thought maybe mile-high sandwiches." He grinned wider.

Wow. She didn't think his smile could get any

better. Boy, was she wrong. The killer smile he was giving her was downright swoon-worthy. And, good grief, could he fill out a pair of jeans.

"We could even have twoooo sammiches." He wiggled his eyebrows.

She laughed and tucked a piece of hair behind her ear. "That sounds good," she said as she shut the door behind her.

"I've never been anywhere this quiet. Are earmuffs covering the whole house?"

A snort popped out, and her cheeks grew hot enough to blister. She peeked at him, but he was still smiling at her like it was no big deal. Jacob would have made fun of her. "And dark. Living in Orlando, it's never this dark."

His lips parted. "Right?"

"I can't see my hand in front of my face."

"I've stubbed my toe so many times I think I need a cast."

Livy laughed harder than she had in a long time. "Well, that makes me feel better. I ran into the wall the first night here."

"You did?"

"Hurt my nose and pride, but that was about it."

They entered the kitchen, and Gabe began pulling meat, cheese, and vegetables from the fridge. She wasn't sure what kind of sandwich he was going to make, but with everything he was pulling out, it was going to be huge.

"I just had a thought," he said.

"What's that?"

"I make the sandwich, and we share it."

She leaned against the counter. "I could slice the tomato and break off the lettuce."

"Okay, but you'll share?"

"Sure."

Livy found a cutting board and knife and began slicing the tomato. With a side-glance, she saw him layering deli meat and cheese. Just how big was he going to make this sandwich? He did say he wanted to share, but she hadn't expected an entire deli case between two slices of bread.

"I'd try to do this with Rachelle, but she wouldn't have anything to do with it. If it wasn't made by the finest chef, it was *beneath* her palate."

Keeping quiet, she kept her attention on her task. She'd have to assume Rachelle was the reason behind his sadness. Livy could be wrong, but she suspected she wasn't.

The simple stuff was what she enjoyed. Someone who just wanted a walk on the beach or to take a drive without knowing the end destination. It wasn't about the what. It was about the who.

"My dad and I would do this. Make this huge sandwich and then cut it in half and share it. Every time I tried to show her just a little glimpse of who I really was, she wanted nothing to do with it. I was never good enough." He froze and covered his mouth with his hand, keeping his gaze pinned on the sandwich. "I don't think I've ever said that aloud," he whispered.

With a nod of her head, she cut the last slice and began working on the lettuce.

"I...Rachelle and I ran in the same social circles. Both our families had money, but mine was a little higher on the social scale."

Livy glanced at him, encouraging him to continue.

Gabe grabbed a couple of slices of tomato and set them on top of the pile of meat and cheese. "People just expected us to be together, so that's what we did. Over time, I fell in love with her, but she loved herself just as much, and there was no room for me."

She handed him a few lettuce leaves, and he placed them on the sandwich and topped it with bread. Then he picked up the knife and cut it down the middle, plating one half for each of them. He slid the plates onto the bar next to each other and walked to the stools with her following.

If he wanted to talk more about Rachelle, she wouldn't stop him, but she wasn't going to comment on anything he said. What was there to say? He loved someone, and they hurt him.

As she slipped onto the barstool, she looked at the sandwich. It was the biggest she'd ever seen. In her mind, she was thinking a t-shirt or some sort of recognition should be awarded if she managed to finish it. There was no way she was even getting her mouth around the thing.

With a quick glance, she saw him take a giant bite. Did his jaw unhinge or something?

Livy picked up the sandwich and managed to get half of it in her mouth. The flavors worked together so well it made her moan. It was incredible. "This is so good," she said as she covered her mouth while she chewed.

"Sandwich-making is an art."

"I'd say so. How did you know to layer it like that?" She took another bite, this time from a different angle. It was just as good as the first.

He shrugged. "Experimenting. My dad and I did this every Saturday at lunch. My brothers and sister all had things they attended, and I didn't. He did something special with all of us. This was just our thing." He took another bite of his sandwich.

She would have given anything to have that. "What did he do with your siblings?"

Finishing the bite, he said, "Well, my oldest brother, Brenden, loved anything sports, so they'd play basketball every week. My other brother, Peter, loved horses, so they'd go riding. And my baby sister, Kath, loved opera, so they'd find a Broadway show to watch. It was his way of staying connected with us. I lost him two years ago. He had a heart attack. One minute he was fine, and the next…"

Her heart broke for him. In all her dreams, she had someone wonderful who loved her. Someone who wanted to spend time with her and be connected. "He sounds wonderful. Is your mom okay?"

He stared at her a moment and then answered, "She's better. We all took it hard. My baby sister lost her way for about nine months, but she's slowly remembering who she was and what he wanted for her."

"I can't imagine the grief she must have felt," she said as she pulled a piece of roast beef off her sandwich and nibbled it. "I loved my dad, and I have all these fuzzy memories of him. Hers were probably crystal clear, and I bet it was a thousand tiny cuts every time she passed a marquee." The first few months after she lost her parents, she cried every night.

"Do you have any clear memories of him or them?"

She smiled. "Yeah, the last Christmas we had. It was in front of the fireplace."

"You lived in Florida, and you had a fireplace?"

Nodding, she said, "Yeah, but it didn't get used very much. That year we did. It was really cold for Christmas, and it even snowed."

"That's why you enjoy sitting in front of the fire."

"The smell reminds me of it."

He put his elbow on the bar and then his head in his hand. "Did you ever find a foster family that wanted to keep you?"

"I did. I only had two years, and they were nice people, but I didn't fit in. We stayed in touch for a while after I aged out, but over time, we just stopped communicating." She paused and looked at her sandwich. "I think this will be my three daily meals for at least the next two days."

Gabe laughed and sat back. "It was less about the food—"

"And more about the connection."

He nodded. "Yeah."

She nibbled a little more on the sandwich. "It sounds like you have a wonderful family."

He nodded. "I do."

Livy slid off her stool as Gabe stood, and they crashed into each other. She wobbled, and his hands gripped her elbows to steady her. When she looked up, all rational thought drained out of her ears. Butterflies were moving so fast that her stomach felt dive-bombed.

Gabe held her gaze, and her lungs screamed for air. She stepped back and hid her shaking hands behind her back. "I'll get the kitchen cleaned up."

"I can help."

She turned and quietly sucked in a lungful of air as she started the dishes. Holy smokes, was that intense. Jacob hadn't ever elicited that strong of a response in her. The snow needed to stop, and those snowplows needed to get there pronto. Her little nutso heart couldn't take much more.

"Have you been able to get any information on the snowplows? All I get is 'keep checking back,'" Livy said, trying to keep her voice steady.

"Same. With that snowstorm slowing down and dumping more than they predicted, it could be a while. They'll clear out major roadways before they ever get here."

"Oh."

"Are you disappointed?"

"Oh, no. I was just curious. I know you wanted space, and I can't leave until I can drive out of here."

He stopped drying the dishes and took her hand. "I told you if you weren't here I'd be going crazy. This snowstorm is working in my favor."

Little zings zipped up her arm and lassoed around her. "Okay." Man, was Gabe something. How could such a little touch make her brain foggy?

When he let her go, he returned to what he was doing, and she braced herself against the counter. Oh yeah, those snowplows needed to get there, or her heart was going to be toast.

*a*s the fire crackled in the fireplace, Livy curled her legs under her on the couch. With her laptop in her lap, the blank screen was a banshee screaming at her. She'd written sentence after sentence, only to erase it. Nothing was coming out right.

Emily needed her beginning so she could meet Xavier. There couldn't be a happily ever after if the stinking beginning never happened. She leaned her head back against the couch and groaned. What was wrong with her brain that she couldn't write? Why weren't the words coming to her? What she'd clung to before was abandoning her when she needed it the most.

How could she forget the world she was living in if

she didn't create something better? She set the laptop next to her on the couch and put her face in her hands. Why was this so hard? Because love wasn't fair, and the heart could be really stupid.

Jacob was a jerk. A low-down-dirty-rotten guy. He'd treated her horribly, and yet, she still ached for him. What did she have to do to let go of what happened to her? *Face it, duh,* her head said. Her heart stuck its fingers in its ears and gave her head a raspberry. If she could just get them together and work it out, she could get back to writing.

Why had she let him treat her so badly for so long? She wished she could be different, but every time she tried, she felt awful. People make mistakes. Not forgiving them for making a stupid decision was wrong in her mind. She'd made mistakes, and she understood that sometimes a person's brain just doesn't fire when it should.

"Having a hard time?" Gabe asked. His deep voice was caramel for the ears. She could imagine her eardrums grinning.

She lifted her head and nodded. "I can't do it."

"Write?"

"Yeah, I can't." Her bottom lip trembled, and she caught it between her teeth to still it.

Gabe walked to the chair that was to the left of her and sat. "Want to talk about it?"

Her stomach twisted in knots, and she looked away. This was her chance. Where was her voice?

"I told you a little about Rachelle yesterday."

Livy nodded.

"She was gorgeous. Long blonde hair, crystal-green eyes, tall. She had a stint as a runway model."

Livy's heart dropped, and she was fumbling to pick it back up. Now she was certain she was nowhere near his league. Just as well. With that fact firmly in place, there was no room for speculation or what-if's.

"That's where it ended. Oh, she was great at playing the part of caring and sweet. She certainly had me fooled. Even my father thought she was amazing. Oh, I'd hear little things from time to time. She spat at a waiter, tripped another woman she considered a rival, put gum in someone's hair…but women envied her, so it was easy to just dismiss it as jealousy-fueled rumors."

Livy tilted her head. How did such a horrible woman get a great guy like Gabe and not appreciate what she had?

"And she was intelligent and driven. Top of her class at Harvard Law, Dean's List. Not that she wanted to use the degree. That wasn't her plan at all. She was going to marry into wealth. The degree was just for clout." He crossed his ankle over his knee. "If there was a picture of the perfect woman, it was her. And a perfect example of a picture not being all that it seems."

Geez, that was perfection? Maybe Livy didn't want that after all.

"It wasn't long after my dad died that I decided to ask her to marry me. Losing my dad kind of woke me up. Life is short. I wanted a family of my own, and I thought Rachelle did too."

Livy couldn't picture a woman not falling over themselves wanting to be with him.

"I made this grand proposal, including a trip to Italy. She said yes, and over the next year, we planned our wedding. Loads of flowers, a live band, five-star food, a cake that could feed a small country, and we rented a massive venue so everyone could come. There were at least five hundred people in attendance."

Livy's eyes grew wide. Five hundred people? Good gracious. She wasn't sure there were five hundred people she knew, even if she went back to kindergarten.

Gabe smiled and gave her a tight laugh. "It was huge.

It was such a crazy week leading up to the wedding. Rachelle's less-than-great behavior shined through a little, and some of her luster was getting a little dull, but it was right before our wedding. It was stressful, scary, and chaotic. I couldn't say my luster was much better."

Livy didn't believe that for a second. He may have been scared and stressed, but she suspected he had been nothing but kind.

"Our wedding day arrived, and my heart was in overdrive. I was standing at the front of the church, happy and excited. I loved her. I wanted to be with her." He paused and shifted in his seat. "Next thing I knew, her mother was standing next to the minister, and she was whispering in his ear. He looked out at the crowd and announced that Rachelle had called off the wedding."

With a soft gasp, Livy's lips parted, and she covered her mouth with her hand. She thought she'd been hurt by Jacob, but she couldn't imagine getting to the very end and having it called off. It had to have been devastating for him.

Gabe looked down, and his jaw tightened. "The world had splintered under my feet. And all of it happened in front of five hundred people—most I didn't even know. All of these strangers with their eyes trained on me, the looks on their faces ranging from pity to judgment."

Livy pulled her bottom lip in and quickly used the butt of her hand to wipe away a tear streaming down her cheek. He didn't need her pity or sympathy. All he needed was someone to listen.

"That was a year ago, and my migraines started at that point. I've been a wreck longer than I should have been. My brothers, my sister, and my mom circled around me and were a barrier to the outside world until I could get myself together again. Without them, I don't know where I'd be." He looked up, catching her gaze and holding it. "So, I may not look very broken, but I'm not exactly all in one piece either."

That feeling was as familiar as breathing. How long had it been since she'd been in one piece? Part of her had broken when her parents died. Another when her...foster brother left her in the cane fields...she blinked and looked away. No, she'd locked that secret up and thrown away the key. And then Jacob. Broken had become such a central part of her that she couldn't picture how it would be to feel whole.

GABE STUDIED LIVY, wondering if she might open up a

little more. Sharing what happened with Rachelle was a huge step for him. Once that nightmare had been over, he'd vowed to cover it with enough dirt that it would never find its way to the top again. Only, it never really felt buried. It felt more akin to a dark shadow looming over him.

He hadn't even planned on telling Livy. The words had just spilled out. There was something different about her. An invisible rope pulling him toward her. Her spirit was talking to his, and it just felt right.

"Jacob." The name came from her lips in a whisper. "I met him just out of college. He was funny, sweet, and outgoing. He was my complete opposite. I made wallflowers look like party animals. Still do."

He chuckled. Clearly, she didn't know how funny she was.

Her eyebrows knitted together, and she chewed her thumb. "I really…I know it was hard to share that, but…"

"What happened to you can't be any more embarrassing or humiliating than what happened to me."

She shook her head. "You didn't know about Rachelle. She hid who she was from you. At the time, sure, it was humiliating, but can't you see? Her true colors coming out that day saved you even more heartache. Can you picture finding out after you'd been married to her? What if you'd had kids?"

Actually, he'd been so caught up in being hurt that he'd never stopped to think that any part of what happened was good. He'd been publicly dumped in front of a mass audience.

Livy continued. "You were strong. You didn't keep letting her back into your life to reopen that wound time and time again. She didn't lie to you and try to convince you she'd changed. You had a family who loved you to help you pick up the pieces."

He touched his fingers to his lips as he considered her words. She was right. Not about being strong, but about having people who cared about him in the aftermath. Yes, what happened was painful, but his family had been there for him when he needed them most. What would it have been like to have no one? What would it have been like to lose his dad at eight? His mom and siblings? A new appreciation for what he had bloomed in his chest.

When he looked at her, there were so many emotions playing on her face that he couldn't get a read on her.

Stormy gray eyes locked with his. "I should want to tell you. To tell someone, but it's hard for me to do that. People take my weaknesses and use them against me. I'm not sure I'm strong enough to give someone else that chance."

"I wouldn't." Should he just break down and tell her how weak he'd been when it came to Rachelle? That no matter how much his head explained that she was no good, his heart still tried to hang on to the years they'd had together, making it hard to let go of the hope that she'd change.

Livy closed her laptop and stood. "I promise what you've told me will never leave my lips, but...I can't. I don't know you, and even if I did, I'm not sure I can trust myself anymore."

Gabe came out of his chair and faced her. "I'll show you that you can trust me."

Tears pooled in the corners of her eyes. "I think that space I came for would be a good thing right now." Without another word, she nearly ran from the living room, and he heard the door shut.

He raked his hand through his hair and walked to his room. All he wanted to do was help, and he'd driven her away. Why had he pushed so hard? Now she wanted space.

His shoulders sagged. He didn't want space. If anything, the more he got to know her, the less space he wanted.

They'd taken a million steps back. What was he

going to have to do to get her to walk back? He was the CEO of a billion-dollar company. Surely he could think of something to get them back to at least talking again. What could he do in a frozen tundra with no way out?

CHAPTER 9

*L*ivy's ringing phone pulled her out of her dream, and she answered it. That didn't happen very often. "Hello?" she mumbled.

"Liv?" Tori asked.

"Yeah."

"You sound drunk."

She rubbed her eyes with her hands. "I sound tired."

After she left Gabe in the living room, she'd cried her eyes out and fallen asleep. He'd opened up to her, and in response, she'd put up a wall with barbed wire lining. What must he think of her? Sharing something so personal and then being stomped on? What kind of horrible person was she?

"Hey, I just wanted to let you know that I'm pretty

91

sure the rumor is true. Saxon is buying Romero. It's super hush-hush because the Saxon CEO is out of town right now. As soon as he gets back, they'll be making the announcement."

Her heart dropped into her toes. If she didn't have her book done by the time the ink was dry, her career as an author would be over. "Oh boy. What am I going to do?"

Tori took a deep breath. "Livy, I love you, and this is going to be hard to hear."

Livy braced herself for one of Tori's not-so-peppy pep talks.

"Just how much of your life do you want Jacob controlling? Do you really want him to take away something you love because you can't put him behind you?"

"I don't want him to control any of my life. I want to be free of him. That's why I changed my phone number and moved apartments. He was so much a part of my life for so long—"

"And I know that. Look, I get it. Your childhood was a nightmare, and you have trouble letting words slide off your back, but in this instance, you have to. You are good at what you do. You are a fantastic romance writer, and Jacob shouldn't be allowed to take that from you."

Livy could hear the truth in the words. Why couldn't she just apply them? "I know, and I hear you. I'm trying. Honestly, I am."

"Okay, but while you're doing that, keep in mind that no one knows when this CEO is coming back. You might have a week, maybe two. You've cranked some out that fast before. Dig deep and do it again."

Livy looked over at her closed laptop. Two weeks at most, and she hadn't been able to write a word in a year? How was she going to pull that off? What if she told Gabe just a little? He'd trusted her. "I'll do it. One way or another, I'll do it."

"Good. I'm counting on you. You know that, right?"

Great. Because there wasn't enough pressure already. "I know."

"Don't sound so glum. I have faith in you. I always have, and I always will."

"Thanks, Tori."

"I'll call you if I hear anything else about the buyout."

"Okay, talk to you later."

"Bye," Tori said and ended the call.

Pulling the phone from her ear, she looked at the time. Nine in the evening. She wanted to march right out into the living room while she had her gumption cup running over, but as icky as she felt, she needed a shower first.

Once she was freshly showered and dressed, she paused at the door with her hand on the knob. If she went out there, she couldn't chicken out again. For once, she was going to be a character from one of her novels and do the brave thing.

She squared her shoulders and held her head high as she opened the door, her description on the back cover of her book playing in her head:

Olivia Weber knew only heartbreak, but with weeks left to write her new novel—she needed her heart mended enough that the words would flow again. Would Gabe Andrews be the key to her freedom? Or would it just be another jail cell?

In her mind, she erased the last sentence. No, it wouldn't be another jail cell. She strolled down the hall and into the living room, pausing by a chair as she took in Gabe on his back, stretched out asleep in front of the fireplace.

One hand was laid across his chest, and the other was behind his head. He'd put on a solid-blue long-sleeved shirt and dark-wash jeans. Boy, was he ever gorgeous. She looked down at the goofy pajamas she'd put on. A change of clothes was in order.

As she turned, he said, "Don't leave again."

She quickly turned around. "I was just going to change clothes."

"Why? You look great." He yawned and sat up, rubbing his face with his hands.

"Well, I…it seems to be all I wear." It took a second for her brain to catch up. Did he say she looked great? Had she gone past delirium and into hallucination?

He chuckled. "Isn't this supposed to be a getaway? Aren't you supposed to wear what you want and be comfortable?"

That was a good point.

"How about you come over here and sit down? You owe me for ditching me all day. I've been bored to death."

Livy smiled and touched her fingers to her lips. She walked over and sat cross-legged next to him. "I'm sorry for running away."

"If I said sorry for every time I ran away, it would be the only word in my vocabulary."

GABE COULD HAVE fist-pumped the air if it wouldn't have made him look like a nutcase. He'd waited all day for Livy to come back out. And he hadn't been lying about being bored out of his mind either. He'd checked for sleds all over the house, and there wasn't one. If he ever came back, they were going to be on his shopping list.

She fidgeted with the hem of her shirt a moment. "I met Jacob one night at a party on the beach."

His heart pounded. He'd hoped like crazy that she'd come back and open up to him. The little flicker of a flame he'd felt earlier burned a little brighter, and it nearly choked him. He tamped the fire down. There didn't need to be any fires flickering for Livy. This was just getting to know each other. What else was there to do until the snowplows came?

"It wasn't something I normally attended, but Tori was in town, and she wanted to do something fun. Tori isn't exactly a movies-and-popcorn kind of girl."

He laughed. "No, she doesn't strike me as that."

"Anyway, he was with a group of friends. They were surfers, and we all started talking. Well, Tori talked, and I brushed up on my wallflower skills." She took a deep breath. "He took an interest in me when I kept quiet. No one had ever done that before. Seen me. I was always…blendable."

Man, she had no idea how wrong she was.

"I don't know if it was insta-love, but it was defi-nitely insta-like. As I said, he was my opposite. I wanted his carefree, throw-himself-into-the-world attitude to rub off. I wanted to not care what people thought about me.

"At first, we were just friends. That's it. Over the next two years, we became inseparable. We were really good friends, and eventually, that led to dating. I fell in love with him. He knew…most of my secrets, and I knew all of his. Only, he'd left out the biggest secret. The one where he was dating three other women at the same time that he was seeing me."

What a jerk. Gabe couldn't stand cheaters.

Continuing, she tucked a piece of hair behind her ear and said, "We had a huge fight and broke up. A few months later, he showed up at my door with an armful of roses and an apology that could've been written by Shakespeare. It was so sweet, and it felt so genuine."

"But it wasn't?"

She shook her head. "He was surfing at a competition in Hawaii. I wanted to surprise him, so I flew over, and when I knocked on his hotel room, a woman answered it wearing his shirt. I raced out of that hotel and flew home. I was done."

A tear streaked down her cheek, and she caught it with the butt of her hand. "I didn't answer his calls or texts, and he showed up at my door yet again. This time swearing it wasn't what I thought. That I was the only one for him. That the girl who answered the door was his buddy's girlfriend, and that t-shirt she had on looked similar to his because his friend had been in the same surf competition."

Gabe's heart hurt for her. He knew exactly how she felt. Rachelle had done similar things to him. Throwing him away, only to return, saying she'd changed her mind again.

Livy stopped and licked her lips. "I bought it. I knew who he was talking about, and they did surf a lot in the same competitions. For the next five months, everything was great, or so I thought." Her voice cracked.

"He asked me to marry him, and I said yes." She bumped Gabe's shoulder with hers. "It wasn't Italy, but it was romantic. Flowers, an incredible dinner, and a balloon ride where he got on one knee. It was...I could've written it; it was so perfect."

Covering her hand with his, he squeezed it. It felt as though her heart was speaking to his and they were comparing notes on heartache.

"The next time I caught him with a woman, he couldn't deny what I saw. He was in a bar with her in full view of everyone and making out with her. I was crushed. I'd been so stupid to believe him." Tears streamed down her cheeks. "After that, I was done. We were done, but it felt like I was cutting out a piece of myself. I loved him."

Gabe wanted so badly to put his arm around her. That Jacob guy was a class A moron and had no idea what he'd thrown away. "That's why you've had such a hard time writing?"

With a small nod, she said, "Looking back, I should have wised up sooner. He was mean to me. Not physically, but he'd call me names. Tell me I was fat or stupid. He said he was just joking, even after I told him how much it hurt me."

If Gabe ever met Jacob, the guy was going to leave with a black eye. It wasn't right to treat people like that, especially someone like Livy.

"I want to write again. I love it, but for some stupid reason, I can't."

"You said you can't miss another deadline, right?"

She nodded. "Tori called me earlier. There's a rumor that another publisher is buying mine. She said they don't keep authors who miss their deadline, and I've got maybe two weeks at most."

Inwardly, Gabe growled. No one was supposed to leak that. The next time he spoke to his mom, he'd let her know someone had talked.

"Maybe it's not as bad as you think," he said.

"Or maybe it's worse. I could have only one week,

and I have no idea what to do. I thought maybe… talking would help clear my head enough that I could at least get started."

He smiled. That's why she'd confided in him. He drew his knees up to his chest and wrapped his arms around them. "Want to know what I think?"

Livy's big gray eyes locked with his. "Yes."

"I think that Jacob guy was insane. You are kind, sweet, and funny. You're the best listener I've ever met. You don't talk over people or try to push them to do something they don't want to do. And you share sandwiches with them when they've bitten your head off only a few hours earlier."

A smile spread on her perfectly pink lips, and she looked away as a blush blanketed her cheeks.

"And before you go worrying about whether I mean it or not, I mean it. Every word." He stretched his legs in front of him and braced his hand on the floor behind her as he leaned toward her. "You are a beautiful, intelligent woman, and a man with any kind of brains would be stupid to let you go."

She glanced at him. "I don't know what to say."

"You don't have to say anything. Just receive it as truth."

"Thank you," she whispered. "For listening…and for the…the sweet compliment."

Gabe risked putting his arm around her and pulled her close. "Thank you for keeping me company."

She leaned her head against his shoulder, and the peace that came over him convinced him that the universe had finally aligned. Just him, someone he cared about, and a simple fire. No fancy dinner, jewels, or events. Just them.

Rachelle had broken his heart, but the woman sitting next to him was making it worth it. Maybe it was time he started looking at that whole situation in a different light.

CHAPTER 10

*G*abe's phone rang, dragging him out of a deep sleep. He grumbled and put it to his ear. "Mom?"

"No, darling."

Rachelle. He looked at the time. Of course she'd call at nearly midnight. When did she ever have any concern for anyone else? He'd told her not to call... with as much conviction as he could muster at the time. He was annoyed at hearing her voice, and it caught him off guard. Why was she calling now? She always did this. Just when his head and heart got on the same page, she'd call...he could time her. He rubbed his face with his hand. "What do you want, Rachelle?"

"Testy. Who's got your boxers in a bunch?"

He took a deep breath to calm himself and sat up. He was fully awake now. "No one. Why are you calling?"

"I heard Millie sent you to the middle of Nowhere, Montana. I felt sorry for you. Thought I'd call and cheer you up."

Right. That wasn't possible. Nothing about Rachelle even remotely cheered him up. "Oh yeah?"

"Of course. Why wouldn't your best girl call to check on you?"

If he didn't know her so well, it would sound sincere, but since he did, he knew it was more sarcasm than anything. Why had he stayed with her so long? What had possessed him to even want things to work between them?

He shook his head. "You're not my best girl anymore, Rachelle. You haven't been since you left me at the altar." He'd never said it with so much conviction, and it had come from so deep inside that he knew he was done for good this time.

"You've never spoken to me so harshly before."

"You're right. I haven't, but I should have."

She scoffed. "Darling, what's gotten into you?"

Gabe rubbed his face with his hand. "I'm not your darling. We're done."

"Done? What do you mean?" The lift of her voice gave him a picture of her shocked expression.

"Just what I said. Done. You had your chance." And he was as shocked as she was. Where was it coming from? Livy floated to mind, and he shook his head. It couldn't be her. He was just tired of dealing with his ex. "For some crazy reason, I thought that one day maybe you'd change. That you'd care about me, but you won't. I'm done waiting for you to change. I'm done, period. We're done." He tapped the end call button and looked at the phone in complete bewilderment.

His whole body vibrated as the adrenaline pumped through him. He'd done it. Gabe chuckled. His mom had been right. Talking about it with someone had helped. Not someone. Livy. She was what was different. Hearing her perspective had helped.

The part of his life involving Rachelle and waiting for her had finally come to an end, and he'd never felt better or happier. His heart was finally agreeing with what his head had been pleading all along, and he was free.

He yawned and set his phone down. As exhausted as he was, he was even more thirsty. He crossed the room, opened his door, and stopped as he reached the hall. Why did it have to be so blasted dark in the cabin?

He slid his hand along the hallway wall, feeling for the light switch. He could have sworn it was on the left, right in the middle, but he had yet to find it. Thinking he was at the end, he turned and smacked right into the corner of the wall, which landed him on his rear end so fast and hard that it knocked the wind out of him. For a second, it also felt like his wits had been knocked out of him too, and he shook his head.

A door opened, and the light switched on. He heard a sharp inhale and then he felt Livy's presence next to him. Even a bump to the head couldn't lessen his awareness of her.

"Oh my goodness. What happened?" she asked as slender fingers touched his forehead. "You're bleeding."

"I used my face to find the corner of the wall." He winced as he touched the cut, and his fingers brushed hers. The touch sent another jolt of awareness through him.

She put her arm around his waist. "Let me help you up, and I'll see if I can find a first aid kit."

He put his arm around her shoulders and used the wall to pull himself up. With her help, he made it to the chair in the living room and sat down hard.

"I'll be right back," she said as he leaned his head against the back of the chair and closed his eyes.

The left side of his head pounded. If he didn't get it under control fast, he wouldn't be able to function for a while.

Air moved, and he opened one eye.

Livy perched on the chair arm, set a first aid kit in his lap, and began using a damp cloth to clean the cut. "You might have a scar from this."

"Is it strategically placed?"

She laughed. "What?"

"If it's strategically placed, I can still pass as attractive."

He thought he heard her mumble, "That's not a problem," and heat crept up his neck. He couldn't remember the last time he'd blushed because of a compliment.

She cleared her throat. "I think you'll manage." When she finished cleaning the cut, she dug in the kit for a bandage. "You really whacked yourself good. Do you have a headache?"

"The beginning of one."

"Let me get you something. My foster mom would drink something with caffeine in it. Does that work for you?"

Closing his eyes, he nodded, and his head pounded harder. No more nodding for him.

"I'll be right back."

A few moments passed, and she returned, taking her seat on the chair arm. She took his hand and placed two pain pills in it and held out a cold soda for him.

"Thank you," he said and washed the medicine down with a big gulp of the drink.

"Do you want to lie down?"

"I just want to sit here for the moment. My stomach is queasy." A soft brush of her hand against his cheek caused his eyes to pop open.

Her eyes were roaming over his face, and her eyebrows were knitted together. The way she was looking at him made him think he was the only thing that mattered. She didn't have anywhere else to be, and he wasn't an inconvenience.

"I'm sorry you hurt yourself," she whispered. "I'll go so you can get rid of that headache."

Gabe didn't want her to go. He liked her being near, even if his head and his heart couldn't get on the same page about her. Before she could move, he grabbed her hand. "I'd prefer it if you stayed. Maybe you can keep me from running into more walls."

"Do you want something to cover your eyes?"

He took another big gulp of the drink, but the pounding in his head didn't ease. "Yeah." He set the soda down on the table next to the chair.

She gave him a small smile. "I'll be right back."

The headache seemed to encompass his entire head. There wasn't a place that didn't throb. He should have used his phone for a flashlight, but he didn't think about it. Grimacing, he pulled himself out of the chair and stretched out on the couch.

A second later, the cushion moved, and he cracked his eyes open.

Livy smiled down at him. "Close your eyes."

He did as she asked, and something weighted pressed against his eyelids. "What is that?"

"It's a sleep mask that I made. It has rice in it to hold the fabric down so light can't get in."

"It feels good." The lack of light and the small amount of weight was already helping.

She took his thumb and started rubbing the tip of it between her fingers. "This is supposed to be for stress headaches, but sometimes it works on regular ones."

The longer she massaged, the less his head pounded. He wasn't sure if it was actually helping or if it was her nearness that made him feel better.

Her fingertips lightly drew across his cheek, and he

nearly pressed his face into her hand. "I don't know what else to do for you," she said softly.

He covered her hand with his. "This works."

After that, she slid off the couch and quietly sat on the floor next to him, holding his hand. She was a silent comfort, and he liked that about her.

As he lay there, he forced everything from his mind and let himself drift to sleep, hoping that when he woke up, his head would feel better and he could spend the evening learning more about her.

LIVY JERKED her head up and looked around. From the bank of windows, she could see a sliver of light poking through the clouds. Maybe those snowplows would get there soon, and then she could get back to Orlando.

Her gaze landed on Gabe, who was still asleep and lying on his stomach. The cut on his forehead went from his hairline to his left eyebrow. She wasn't sure how strategically placed it was, but he was still just as attractive to her. And the more she got to know him, the more good-looking he became.

The phone in her room rang, and she quickly stood, racing to grab it off the nightstand before it woke Gabe up. "Hey, Tori," she said and then looked at the phone. "Jacob?" He FaceTimed her? How? She'd changed her number after the last time. Who could have given it to him?

He shot her one of his knee-weakening smiles. Only, her knees didn't feel as gelatin-like as they normally would have. Why didn't they?

Gabe's face flitted through her mind, and she smiled. She shook her head to clear her thoughts. He was a nice man. That's all.

"Hey, sweetheart," Jacob said.

It felt as though someone was pressing her lungs flat. Her body started shaking, and she quickly sat on the edge of the bed. "Why are you calling me?"

He'd called every few months, but she'd stayed strong each time, telling him no. The last time, she'd changed her phone number. When four months had passed, she was sure he was done, and now, here he was again. Why couldn't he leave her alone?

After her talk with Gabe, she'd actually felt pretty good. She'd even gotten a little writing done. Then she'd heard a thump and found him on the floor bleeding. Talking to Gabe had lifted a huge weight off of her. Then he'd been sweet and complimented her. Her heart had pounded at triple speed.

"I had business to take care of, but you know us. I always come back."

She palmed her cheek as tears pricked her eyes. "I told you last time to never call me again. Why would you do this?" When she got back to Orlando, she was changing her number again and making sure Jacob never got it, ever. And she wasn't letting him take away her ability to write. Not this time.

"You left me at the altar. What's a guy who's madly in love supposed to do?"

Livy clenched her jaw. He always said that like it was somehow going to miraculously be funny one day. "I did *not* leave you at the altar. I left you two days prior to the wedding during rehearsals when I caught you making out with one of hotel staff in the bar. You weren't even hiding it, Jacob."

"Aw, babe, it was just wedding jitters. You know, cold feet." He used the tone she hated. The one where he put the blame on her.

She shook her head. "I don't want to talk about this again. We are done. I can't take it anymore. You hurt me over and over and over, and I took you back every time. Not this time."

"Come on. You know I love you."

Whatever brand of love Jacob subscribed to was one she wanted nothing to do with.

"Livy."

She stared at the screen.

"I've changed. I swear it. There's no one else for me. I love you, Livy."

How many times had they had this exact conversation? "No. I can't do it again. It's not just about cheating on me. Being with you is toxic. You make fun of me, call me names, tell me I'm fat. I can't do it again. I won't."

"They were jokes."

"But they weren't funny."

"You just don't have a sense of humor."

Her shoulders sagged. Why couldn't he understand? And why was she putting up with it? "I'm over you. I deserve better."

"Aw, Liv, come on." His eyebrows squished together, and he was trying to use his big blue puppy dog eyes on her. Not this time.

"I'm done, Jacob." Why was she still on the phone with him? "This is goodbye. Don't call me anymore." She ended the call and curled into a ball on her bed.

The dull ache sharpened, and she hugged herself. She'd promised herself she wouldn't cry over him ever again, but as hard as she tried, she couldn't stop the flow. What was wrong with her that she'd grieve over someone who treated her like dirt?

Why couldn't she have just a little faith in who she was as a person and believe that she was worthy to be loved? Her parents had loved her. She remembered that much. And Gabe seemed to think she was okay. Maybe it was time to start giving herself a little more credit and expect more from people.

She sat up and dried her eyes. What exactly was she crying about? Jacob had been awful to her. It was time to move on.

She'd written a little earlier, and the rush of adrenaline was pumping through her now, giving her a boost. She was over Jacob, and it felt...great. There was a book that needed to be written, and she was going to deliver. But first, she needed to check on Gabe.

CHAPTER 11

Of course, Livy was no different than any other woman. She'd left her fiancé at the altar too. Gabe heard the guy say it. Not that he'd intended to eavesdrop, but once he heard that, he was done and stormed to his room where he shut the door. He'd heard enough.

It just wasn't right to do that to someone. Jacob had hurt her, but she didn't have to be cruel. Had she waited to dump him on their wedding day for spite after finding him making out with the other woman? What was with Gabe and finding women that dumped guys at the altar?

Yeah, he thought Jacob was a jerk, and she should have ditched him. Livy didn't deserve to be treated like that. No one did. But after being left at the altar, he had no tolerance for anyone who did that for any reason. There were other more discreet ways to handle it.

She had ample opportunities to give Jacob the heave-ho without doing in front of an audience. Never leave them when they're standing in front of friends and family. If a person's going to leave, do it before then so it's not as humiliating.

Gabe pulled up the weather app on his phone and checked on the road conditions. "Great," he said and raked his hand through his hair. She'd have to stay at least a few more days, but that was it. The moment he could get that woman out of his cabin and out of his life, the better.

How was he such a horrible judge of character? First Rachelle and now her. Livy hadn't come across like that at all, but he'd heard it. What had the guy done that she couldn't have at least had the decency to stop the wedding before she embarrassed him?

A knock came from the door, and he yanked it open. Anger rushed through him. Her smile greeted him, and had he not overheard her conversation, it would've thrilled him. Now, seeing her made him sick to his stomach.

"Is your headache better?" she asked. She sounded sweet, but now he knew better.

"I think it's best if we go back to our corners for a while. Our distant corners, if you get my drift." He couldn't hide the disdain he had for her.

She blinked and stepped back, confusion written all over her face. "Oh, okay."

Without a word, he slammed the door in her face and paced the floor in front of his bed. He couldn't understand why he was so furious with her. It was disproportionate to the length of time he'd known her. He shouldn't be so out of his mind, but he was.

Gabe stopped pacing and threw himself on the bed. What was going on with him? The answer flashed in neon. He liked her. Okay, so maybe that wasn't exactly the whole truth. Falling for her was more accurate.

Livy was comfortable and easy. Something about her called to him. The way she'd look at him made him feel like she enjoyed his company. They could share a simple sandwich and sit in front of the fire and talk. Things he never could've done with Rachelle. His soul was at rest when she was around.

There was another knock on his door. "Go away, Livy. I want some space." He almost added, "Find somewhere else to be," but for some reason, he held it back. As angry as he was, he wasn't going to be cruel.

He'd been on the receiving end of that, and he'd promised himself he'd never be that way to another human being, no matter who they were.

His phone rang, and he answered it with a sharp, "Hello."

"Gabe?"

He closed his eyes. "Hey, Mom, sorry."

"Is everything okay?"

No, but if he told her anything, she'd try to meddle. His mom would like Livy. Not just because she was his mom's favorite author, either. "Yeah, fine. What's going on?"

"I have news about Albert."

Sitting up, he said, "What's happened?"

"His niece needs a new kidney. They've been having fundraisers, but transplants are expensive, and his brother's family doesn't have insurance."

"I'll pay for it. Whatever she needs. Tell Albert I'm sorry. Why didn't he come to me? To us?"

His mom sighed. "He didn't want to come to his boss and tell him all of his problems."

Gabe raked a hand through his hair. "He's not just an assistant. He's...he's family. We take care of family. Is there anything else they need?"

"I don't know. He broke down when I asked him

about it, and after that, I didn't get much other than information about his niece."

"He should have just come to us. Find the hospital where she's staying and tell them we'll take care of the bill and anything else they need. Then find her pharmacy and tell them any medication is to be billed to me."

"I'll go in half with you. From what little I can gather from the pictures on his desk, the family has been struggling for more than a year."

And Gabe had been so caught up in his own world that he didn't even notice. He swore under his breath. "We'll take care of whatever they need."

"Your dad would be so proud of you, but not half as proud as I am. All four of you. Brenden found out, and he's offered to fix their roof. Paul is getting Hannah a tutor because she's missed so much school. And Kath is going to be running errands for them."

Gabe smiled. His baby sister was one of the kindest people he'd ever met. *Livy.* Her name felt whispered in his ear. He pushed the thought away. "It's right up her alley."

"Yeah, it is." He could see his mom's smile, could hear the emotion in her tone.

He searched his mind. There was something he

was supposed to tell her the next time he spoke to her. "Mom, someone's leaked the buyout."

"What?" she snapped.

He raked a hand through his hair. "Livy's agent knows about the buyout. Someone is leaking."

She exhaled sharply. "I'll find out who."

"Good."

Silence hung between them a moment, and he could feel the shift in the conversation. "How's your cabin guest?"

The question was a paper cut. "She's fine." He tried to hide the iciness, but he couldn't.

"Want to tell me what happened?"

"No."

"Gabe."

"Mom, not right now, okay? Just let me simmer, and I'll tell you next time you call." Maybe by then, he'd have a handle on whatever it was brewing inside him. Maybe those snowplows would arrive and he'd actually have some peace, even if that meant darkness and eerie quiet.

She was quiet a little longer than he was comfortable with, but when she finally spoke, she said, "Okay."

Man, was he glad she let it go. "Thank you."

"I love you, sweetheart. I just want you to be happy."

"I know." That seemed to be a mountain he was never going to be able to climb. The summit was always just out of reach. "I'll talk to you later, okay?"

"Yeah, sweetheart, I'll talk to you later."

"Bye." He ended the call and tossed the phone on the bed. All of a sudden, he was flat-out exhausted. Before he knew what was happening, his eyes fluttered shut, and he was gone.

RETURNING TO HER ROOM, Livy shut the door behind her and crawled onto the bed. The way Gabe had looked at her made her wonder what she could have done wrong. He'd slammed the door in her face. She scoured her memory, and for the life of her, she couldn't imagine what it was that made him angry.

Maybe his headache was still bothering him and he just didn't know how he came across. If that was the case, then she'd keep her distance for a while so he could feel better. She needed to write anyway.

She hopped off the bed, grabbed her laptop off the dresser, and returned. With a few pillows to cushion the log headboard, she settled in for a marathon writing session. Telling Jacob she was done, *really* done, had helped her. There was finality in it.

There had been no room for reconciliation this time, and she'd made that abundantly clear. It was the first time she'd been firm. Just changing her number hadn't been enough. She'd needed to stand strong and tell him she was no longer going to accept whatever he gave her. She did deserve better.

A few hours later, Livy smiled as her word count had climbed exponentially. The story was pouring out of her. Her two main characters were getting closer and finding out about one another, and those first sparks of attraction were turning into something more.

That's what she loved about romance. Not the heated moments. She loved the parts that were intimate because someone was laying their heart bare to the other. There was something magical about being that person who didn't flinch away when someone trusted them with all their darkness. Showing someone that just because something bad happened didn't mean nothing good was ever going to happen.

Livy sighed and set the laptop next to her on the bed. Why couldn't she have that in her own life? Jacob had never shown interest in her. Everything was about fun and adventure. It was great. She enjoyed having fun, but she needed someone to want more than just the fun. She needed someone that wanted all of her.

Someone who cared that she couldn't sleep. That she worried.

Slipping off the bed, she rubbed her neck as she walked out of her room. Her stomach growled. Would Gabe want to share another sandwich or maybe finish their leftovers? What if he barked at her again or slammed the door? Could she handle the rejection?

She chewed her thumb as she looked down the hall at Gabe's door. No, she couldn't. If he slammed the door in her face again, she'd be hurt, and being stuck with him would only make it worse.

Her stomach growled again, and she walked to the kitchen to grab the last half of her sandwich. She suspected it would taste even better now that the flavors had time to marry. As she opened the fridge, she saw it was well-stocked and was grateful since she had no idea when they'd be able to get to a store.

Five minutes later, she walked into the living room with a plated sandwich and a glass of water. The fire had died down, and the air had a chill. Even with the place being heated, it couldn't compete with the windows at the back of the house. They made for a great view of the national park the cabin backed up to, but they did nothing when it came to keeping the place warm.

She set her sandwich down and walked to the fireplace to build a fire before she started eating. There were only a couple of logs left. She needed more.

After walking to the glass door, she opened it open and looked to the left. A stack of wood was a couple of feet away. The temptation to zip out and right back played in her mind, but she dismissed it. It was freezing out, and she only had socks on. She had yet to down that juiced leprechaun.

As she stopped by the coffee table, she took a couple of bites of her sandwich and walked to the front door to put her coat and boots on. On the way back, she picked up a log from the fireplace to keep the door propped open just in case it was one of those that lock behind you.

Livy pulled the door open and set the log down before stepping out onto the porch. Fortunately, the overhang was extra-long. A good foot from the door was free of snow, and the wood was dry. She took a deep breath and pulled her coat tighter around her.

It really was a beautiful place. It looked so...pure. All the white snow covered everything in sight. Evergreen trees stood tall, and snow blanketed their branches. If she were a photographer, she'd be bundled up, taking as many photos as she could.

A chill raced down her spine, and she shivered. It was time to make that fire.

She loaded herself up with an armful of wood, and as she got back to the door, her foot caught on a nail sticking up. The wood dumped out of her hands, and she stumbled back, her hands reaching behind her to stop her fall. As her backside hit the deck, her foot kicked the log holding the door open, and the door snapped shut.

Now she was cold, and her butt hurt. This was why she wore her coat. Because she and Murphy were on a first-name basis. She got up, brushed herself off, and tried the door. Leaning her forehead against the pane, she sagged. Locked.

She looked over her shoulder. There was no way, with all the snow, that she was making it to the front door, and even if she did, it was locked too. Then she'd be even more frozen and still locked out.

Her best hope was that Gabe would hear her pound on the door. Maybe whatever had been bothering him would be forgotten and he'd follow her out as he'd been doing the past couple of days.

Livy pounded against the glass. There was no point in yelling, because she knew he couldn't hear her.

Ten minutes went by, and she started shaking. Her body needed to generate some heat, so she began jumping in place. It worked for a few moments, but then the cold settled into her bones. She sat down on the deck, drew her knees to her chest, and pulled her bulky coat to her ankles.

She continued to pound on the door. When one hand got too cold, she'd switch. The longer she sat there, the more exhausted she got.

If Gabe didn't find her soon, she'd be a popsicle.

CHAPTER 12

Gabe moaned as he rolled to a sitting position and searched the bed for his ringing phone. Putting the phone to his ear, he said, "Hello?" His mouth was as sticky as taffy.

When the ringing didn't stop, he pulled it away from his ear and looked it. It wasn't his phone that was ringing.

He set his phone on the nightstand and rubbed his face with his hands. The ringing finally stopped and then started again. Who would be so incessant in calling? And why was the ring so loud? Shouldn't Livy's door be shut?

The phone stopped ringing and immediately rang again. Whoever it was needed to stop.

Grumbling, he stood and walked to Livy's room

down the hall. The door was open, and by the looks of her open bathroom door, she wasn't in there.

Again, the ringing stopped and then started again. Oh, good grief.

Gabe snatched the phone off her nightstand and answered the FaceTime call. Her agent, Tori, appeared on the screen. "Where's Livy?"

"I don't know."

Her lips pressed together in a hard line. "My assistant gave Livy's ex her number. I was hoping he hadn't called yet so I could warn her."

"Oh, he's already called."

"That slimeball."

Gabe rolled his eyes. "He's the slimeball? He said she was the one that left him at the altar."

"When did you hear him say that?"

"I overheard her facetiming him. I wasn't trying to eavesdrop, but he said she did."

Her jaw clenched and unclenched a few times. "She broke it off with him two days before the wedding because, once again, he had his tongue down another woman's throat. Do you know how many times that jerk crawled back to her, promising her the moon and sun, only to break her heart?"

The color drained from Gabe's face. "What?" She hadn't actually left him at the altar.

"That so-called thing running around in a man's body has put her through the wringer more times than she ever deserved. After they broke up, she found out he'd been cheating on her from the moment he called her his girlfriend. He's low-life scum. He was horrible to her. And even if she *had* dumped him at the altar, that jerk would have had it coming."

He pinched the bridge of his nose.

"Where's Livy? She never leaves her phone. I've been trying to reach her for twenty minutes."

Gabe quickly walked out of Livy's room and into the kitchen. A light pounding was coming from the back of the house, and he swept his gaze along the windows to where it landed on a small hunched figure sitting on the deck. "Tori, I have to call you back."

"What's going on?"

He looked at Tori. "I'll call you back." He ended the call and stuck the phone in his pocket as he raced to the back of the house.

Livy's little body was huddled in front of the glass door with her coat pulled around her. He jerked the door open, tossed the logs onto the house floor, and picked her up. The large porch overhang had kept her dry, but her teeth chattered, and her lips were a faint blue. She needed heat and now.

He gently laid her on the floor in front of the fireplace and got the fire going as quickly as he could. Then he kneeled beside her.

Her eyes opened a sliver. "I-I-I n-n-needed w-w-wood."

"I'm going to go get a blanket. I'll be right back."

He ran to his room and returned with his king-size comforter. He held it up to the fire to warm before laying it out on the floor and putting her on top of it.

Kneeling next to her again, he took her face in his hands and said, "Stay with me, Livy."

The only experience he had with hypothermia was from a camping expedition he and his brothers went on in Alaska. One of the other men in the group got separated, and when they found him, he was nearly dead. The group had watched the instructors work to save the man's life, and Gabe was desperately trying to remember what they'd done.

The one thing he knew for certain was that she needed to get her blood flowing again. He pulled her coat and boots off and yanked his shirt over his head. Then he pulled the comforter over them, wrapped his arms around her, and pulled her as close to his body as he could.

He tucked her head under his chin and her icy hands against his chest, and the cold took his breath away. Gabe tightened his hold on her and wrapped his legs around hers as he rubbed her back.

How long had she been out there? What if Tori hadn't called? Mental images of her big gray eyes staring up at him and looking lost began to play in his mind. He'd slammed the door in her face. She could have died, and that would have been the last interaction they had.

Why had he been so ready to write her off? He should have asked her about it instead of storming to his room. He'd heard Jacob say it. Gabe also knew Jacob had treated her terribly. Why did he just assume that what Jacob said was the truth?

Her hands moved against his skin, and he pulled back just enough to look at her. Pushing her hair from her face and neck, his gaze roamed over her.

"My skin hurts," she murmured.

"You're getting your circulation back. It'll get better."

She rubbed her cheek against his chest and let out a soft cry. "It feels like fire ants are biting me."

There was nothing he could do to make it better. "I know. It won't last long." He hoped.

Over the next half-hour, she squirmed as the blood flow returned to her limbs. When she stopped, she slightly cracked her eyes open. "I'm so tired."

"I'll be here when you wake up."

She put her arm around his waist and flattened her hand against his back. "You're so warm."

Not long after, her chest was rising and falling evenly against his.

As she warmed, the danger that her heart could stop diminished. It also allowed his thoughts to move from making sure she was okay to liking how she felt against him. He enjoyed holding her. It was a strange and unnerving feeling.

He'd been so closed off for the last year that even the slightest hint that he might have interest in someone had sent him running. The thought was a slap. Interested in her? He waved off the crazy thoughts. She'd needed his help, and that's what he'd done. Helped her. That was all.

A soft ring came from his pocket, and he maneuvered enough to fish the phone out. Tori was not one for having patience, apparently. He accepted the Face-Time call and whispered, "Hey."

"You said you'd call me back."

"Shhh…" He pulled the phone out so she could see Livy sleeping. "She got locked outside."

Tori's breath caught. "Is she okay?"

"Yeah, she's okay. If you hadn't called, she wouldn't

have been." What if she hadn't been okay? The thought made his heart hurt.

"Gabe, listen to me."

He looked at the screen and wondered what she could be thinking.

Tori pinched her lips together and then pointed her finger at him. "Don't hurt my friend. If you do, I'll come for you and make you regret it."

"I'm only getting her warm."

Tori grunted. "Right. You're falling for her."

Falling for her? No. "I am not," he whispered. "I'm getting her warm."

Livy's agent lifted an eyebrow and looked at him like he was selling snake oil. "She doesn't put herself out there at all. I'm her only friend. People have used and abused her most of her life. She's not fragile by any means, but there's only so much a person can handle before they finally break. Are you getting what I'm saying?"

He could say he wasn't interested in her all he wanted, but deep down he knew the truth. She'd intrigued him from the moment he met her. The truth was that he was glad the snowstorm had hit and she couldn't leave. "Yeah, I get it."

"Good. I'd hate to have to hurt you."

Gabe chuckled. "I'd hate that too."

"Call me when she wakes up."

He nodded. "Okay."

Tori ended the call, and Gabe tossed the phone into the chair.

You're falling for her. Was he? His chest tightened as he looked down at her. He'd just met her. How was that possible?

A little introspection gave him the answer. Tori was right, he was falling for her. It was a light-bulb moment. He felt lighter, happier, when she was around. She made him laugh. He'd been looking for her without even knowing it. Could it be possible she was feeling the same way? Would she forgive him for judging her and being so harsh earlier?

THE DREAM WAS INCREDIBLE. Gabe was holding her, his breath was hitting her cheek, and his man-and-after-shave smell wrapped around her. She wasn't sure why she was having that dream, but it made her smile. Not that she could let herself be interested in him like that. He was way too far out of her league. It sure was nice to be held, though.

Muscle moved under her hand, and her eyes popped open. Was she having a dream within a dream? Her legs were trapped, and her body was molded against his. Her cheek was pressed against the bare skin of his chest, and butterflies danced in her stomach.

"Hey, how are you feeling?" Gabe's breath hit her cheek again, and a tingle swooshed down her spine.

Slowly, she lifted her gaze, and he was staring straight at her. "Um." Her pulse jumped. With his mouth so close to hers, it was hard to make her tongue work.

A smile spread on his lips. "Um? Not sure that qualifies as a response."

"I'm okay," she breathed.

His eyebrows drew together, and he brushed his fingertips across her cheek. "You scared me. What happened?"

Oh, wow. How was she supposed to have a conversation with him when he was making her skin tingle and all she wanted to do was kiss him? She needed to keep her mind off of how close his face was to hers and how she delighted in the feel of his skin against hers. "There wasn't enough wood to make a fire. I stuck a log in the jam so the door wouldn't shut on me, but I tripped and kicked the log out."

"You could've died," he said, squeezing her.

She looked down, and all she could see was a wall

of toned muscle. Her lungs screamed for air. Her body screamed for mercy. And her heart shimmied like almost dying wasn't a bad thing, especially if this was the way she'd go out.

Livy looked back up. "I'm okay."

"Are you hungry? I noticed you didn't finish your sandwich. We could share one again."

That sounded pretty good, but... "Can I ask you something first?"

"Anything."

"You slammed the door in my face. Can you tell me what I did wrong?" she asked as she held his gaze.

A look of pain crossed his face. "My behavior was childish. I didn't mean to overhear you talking to Jacob, but I did. He said you left him at the altar, and I just—"

"I understand." She nodded as she looked down. It made perfect sense that he would be upset at the thought of another man being left at the altar. But hadn't she just decided that she needed to expect more from people, to have a higher standard for how she allowed people to treat her? Gabe *had* been quick to judge her and harsh in his reaction. Just the kind of treatment she should be avoiding. Still, it was hard to shift her mindset that she deserved better.

He tipped her chin back up with his finger. "No.

What I did wasn't okay, and you should never have thought it was you that did something. I was a flat-out jerk. I stopped listening as soon as he said you left him at the altar. I didn't realize you actually left him before the wedding. I should've asked instead of assuming. You shouldn't be okay with being treated like that."

It struck her as interesting that he was saying what she'd just been telling herself, but hearing it come from him meant something and gave her a little confidence that she was right. She'd never felt such support from a man, and she found it went a long way toward convincing her that she really did deserve better. She also knew Gabe. He wouldn't have treated her like that if it hadn't hit so close to his own hurt. He was a good man with a gentle heart.

She shook her head. "What happened to you makes you want to protect other people from getting hurt. It wasn't great having the door slammed in my face, but you weren't being cruel. You were being sympathetic. Jacob may have hurt me, but just because someone is a jerk doesn't mean I have to respond in kind."

"How do you do that?"

"Do what?"

Gabe cupped her cheek. "You have this peace about you. Like the world hasn't invaded your soul. You can still look at people and see the good in them. How do you do that?"

That was a hard question to answer. She wasn't sure she was ready to tell him why. "It's a strength and a weakness. I always try to find the positive in a situation, even though I've realized recently that sometimes it becomes a way to justify bad behavior. Yes, it gives me peace and allows forgiveness." She paused. "But I'm beginning to realize that it's become a crutch. A way to excuse the way people treat me because I don't deserve better."

"You do deserve better. Better from everyone, and especially from me. I won't do it again. You have my promise on that."

With a small nod, she said, "Okay."

"Can you tell me what caused you to make excuses for people?"

She shrugged. "I don't know. It was a promise I made myself a long time ago."

With the way he looked at her, she wondered if he'd press it, but then he nodded. "Okay. Maybe soon you can tell me how that promise came to be?"

"Maybe."

Gabe hugged her. "You have no idea how glad I am that you're okay." His lips moved against her earlobe, and she giggled.

When he pulled back he was grinning. "Ticklish?"

"Yeah, I'm horribly ticklish."

He smiled, making her wonder if the confession would one day bite her in the rear. "How about I make that sandwich?"

She nodded. "Okay." Whoa. Gabe was taking her emotions in all sorts of directions.

He threw the covers off and untangled himself from her. As he stood, he pulled her up with him. "You okay to walk?"

Livy took a step, and her knees held. "I think so."

Even with the assurance that she could walk, he kept his arm around her waist until they got to the bar. "You sit while I make it. We've still got sliced tomato from the other day."

A ringing came from the living room, and Gabe tapped his forehead. "Oh man, that's Tori."

"Tori?"

"I'll explain after you talk to her." He jogged to the living room, grabbed her phone and his shirt, and returned. "Don't let her kill me," he said as he pulled on his shirt and handed her the phone.

Livy laughed. "I promise I'll protect you." If he talked to her earlier, Tori must have been the one to clarify about leaving Jacob at the altar. She answered the phone. "Hello."

"Oh, thank God you're okay. I was worried sick. Gabe was supposed to call me when you woke up. When I see him—" Her voice was so loud that Livy held the phone away from her ear.

She looked at Gabe, and he grimaced and mouthed, *Sorry.*

"I just woke up."

"He said you got locked outside."

"Yeah."

"For how long?"

She shrugged as she drew circles with her fingers on the top of the bar. "I don't know. I just remember being cold and tired."

"I called you a little after one, and now it's after ten. You've been asleep this entire time?"

In his arms, apparently. "Yeah."

"I guess it would be easy to sleep with him holding me."

Livy needed to think quick. If not, Tori was going to have her wanting to crawl in a hole. "He was just making sure I was okay. That's all. Being that cold can make you go into shock."

After a moment of silence, Tori said, "If you say so." The way she said it, Livy could almost see the smile on her face. "I know Jacob called. Are you okay?"

"Yeah, I'm fine. I need to change my number again.

I don't know how to get him to leave me alone. I did tell him that it was over. Like, over, over. I'm thirty percent done with the new book too."

Tori gasped. "Maybe instead of beating Gabe up, I need to kiss him."

Livy jerked her attention to Gabe. Surely he hadn't heard that. If he did, he was hiding it well. "Um."

She laughed. "Mmmhmm. Definitely need to kiss him."

Covering her burning cheek with one hand, she said, "Shut up."

A flicker of a smile crossed Gabe's lips, and then it was gone.

Yep, Livy needed a hole to crawl into. "I'm going now."

"I want to see some chapters, okay?"

"Sure, later I'll email what I've got so far."

"I can't wait to read it. I'll talk to you tomorrow. Give Gabe a kiss for me for saving my friend."

She groaned. "Tori, stop."

"What? I can't thank the gallant hero for saving my best friend's life?"

"Sure, just don't volunteer my—" She almost said lips. Oh, she needed that hole to crawl into right now.

Tori cackled. "Your what?"

Livy palmed her forehead and groaned. "Goodbye, Tori."

How was she going to look him in the eyes now? She was pretty sure he'd heard the entire conversation. That's what happened when she was friends with someone who'd never learned to use their inside voice.

A plate slid in front of her. "I used olive oil and red wine vinegar on this one to give it a little bit of a different flavor. I would have asked if you liked that, but I didn't want to interrupt," Gabe said.

Slowly, she lifted her gaze to his to say thank you, and he was smiling the most fantastic smile she'd ever seen. He'd definitely heard Tori. Her cheeks burned painfully hot. "Thank you for the sandwich."

He held her gaze. "You're welcome."

Just how much longer was she going to be trapped in this cabin with him? She blew out a big breath and took a bite of the delicious sandwich, glad she had something to stuff her face with so she didn't end up saying something stupid or embarrassing. Those snowplows needed to pick up the pace before her heart forgot he was out of her league.

CHAPTER 13

*L*ivy swallowed the bite as Gabe took a seat next to her. "Tori said thank you for helping me."

"Is that all she said?"

"Yep."

"Are you sure?"

She looked at him, and he had a goofy grin and a twinkle in his eye. He was messing with her. "You heard every word, didn't you?"

"Only the good parts."

She groaned. "Oh, stop."

"Hey, she had a point. I did save your life."

"Yeah, and…"

He grabbed the bottom of her stool and pulled it closer. "And…what?"

Livy slipped off the other side. "I need to go work on my book."

"I thought you were hungry."

"Uh, no. I'm good." Her stomach growled. Was the universe ever going to take pity on her? Just once?

One eyebrow slowly rose. "Oh, really? Does your stomach know that?"

"No, apparently not." She sat down again.

"Now," he said and tapped his cheek. "I believe your agent said something about giving me a kiss."

Her stomach did a flip. Was she really going to give him a kiss on the cheek?

He closed his eyes and tapped his cheek again. "I'm waiting."

She rolled her eyes and inwardly grumbled, promising to do horrible things to Tori the next time she saw her. Leaning over, every hair on her body was standing on end. Goosebumps lined her arms, and nervous energy coursed through her. She pressed her lips to his cheek, and it was a lightning strike that traveled from her head to her toes.

Her eyes closed, and his scent wrapped around her. How could he smell so good all the time?

She pulled back a fraction and lingered. Would it be wrong to kiss him twice? Before she could decide, her body did it for her, and she touched her lips to his cheek again.

Livy leaned back and locked her gaze on the sandwich in front of her. Her head was dizzy, and all she'd done was kiss his cheek. Oh man, she wanted more. "Thank you for coming to my rescue."

"You're welcome." His voice was husky, and she glanced at him. He took her hand in his. "It would upset me if something happened to you."

Gulp. Like an old Batman TV show caption, the word smacked her in front of her eyes. Her heart fluttered, and then her feet touched the ground. He was just being nice. It was an emotionally charged moment. That was all. It didn't matter that her body wanted to lean into him as if he were the sun and she were a flower needing his rays.

They sat in silence, eating their meal together, and then worked to clean up. It struck her as interesting at how well they moved together. It didn't take any verbal communication. They had a rhythm that seemed to speak of years and not days.

Once they were finished, Livy walked out of the kitchen toward her room, but Gabe grabbed her hand and pulled her to a stop. "Are you going to hide in your room?"

"I was going to go work on my book, or at least try."

"Can you do it in the living room?"

She tilted her head. "I can, but I thought after putting up with me for so long that you'd want some space."

Something flashed across his features, and his dark eyes locked with hers. "You aren't nearly as difficult to put up with as you think."

Her lips parted, and her brain stuttered. "Um."

"So, will you sit in the living room?"

No. Then she nodded her head as if it had no direct communication with her brain at all. "Sure," she squeaked and then cleared her throat. "I'll get my laptop and be right out."

The smile he shot her made her knees wobble.

He let her hand go, and she tried to hide that she was nearly stumbling to her room. She paused as she picked up her laptop and thought about changing her mind. She didn't need to get closer to him. He was just bored, and she was the only one to give him company. If she wasn't careful, she was going to get her heart broken by Gabe Andrews. She wasn't sure she could survive another heartbreak so soon after Jacob. Plus, she had a feeling getting caught up in Gabe would be a whole new level of ache.

Grabbing her laptop, she shook her head. He *wasn't* interested in her. Tomorrow morning, everything would be back to normal. He was worried she might still be dealing with side effects of nearly freezing to death. That's all.

Livy walked into the living room, and he was sitting in the chair with his ankle crossed over his knee, staring intently at his phone. She took a seat at the end of the couch furthest from him. He might want her in the living room, but that didn't mean he wanted her all that close.

He looked up from the phone, frowned, and then returned his gaze to his phone.

For the next few hours, she worked on her book while Gabe kept his attention on his phone. Every so often, he'd chuckle, and she'd quickly glance at him. She had no idea what could possibly be so fascinating for that long until he popped out of the chair and sat next to her.

"You're an excellent writer," he said.

She saved her document, sent the first half of the book to Tori, and set the laptop on the side table next to her. "What?"

"I just finished your last book. It was great. The characters were likable and relatable. Your wit shines through in your dialogue. The story itself wasn't just fluff. It had great depth to it."

He read *To Save a Heart*? Jacob never read a word she wrote. "That's what you were doing?"

"I figured you'd be writing and I'd need something to do so I didn't bug you. I loved it."

She smiled, and the giddiness went all the way to her core. He loved it? "I can't believe you read it."

"I'll be reading the rest of them too." He put a little distance between them, and then his leg bounced. "I need to tell you something." He lowered his gaze to his hands.

"Okay." She twisted in the seat toward him and drew her leg under her.

"I'm a little afraid to tell you, to be honest. I don't want you to be angry with me."

She knitted her eyebrows together. "It takes a lot to make me angry."

Gabe kept his head down. "My last name isn't Andrews. I didn't know who you were when I first got here, and when you asked my name, I gave you my mom's maiden name."

Livy laughed. "Okay."

"My last name is Saxon."

Saxon?

"As in Saxon Publishing."

Her jaw slowly dropped. "Sax—"

"You don't need to worry. Your career is safe. I'll make sure of it. With what I just read, there's no way I'd lose you as an author." He finally looked at her.

When she didn't say anything, his shoulders sagged. "I should have told you, and I'm sorry I didn't."

"So, Saxon *is* buying Romero?" She'd been with Romero since the beginning of her career. They'd taken a chance on her, and she felt a little sad that they'd no longer be her publisher.

"Yes. I'm so sorry I didn't tell you sooner. You were worried, and I could have put you at ease, but I didn't. I liked being just Gabe to you."

She shrugged. "You're still just Gabe to me." If they were more than friends, she'd be worried. He was a billionaire. A successful CEO in a city too big for her. A city filled with women way more confident and better suited for dating him. Even if the thought of him being with someone made her ache. It was all crazy anyway. As if he'd really be interested in her.

"You aren't mad?"

"You didn't know who was standing on the other side of the door. Honestly, it kind of makes me wish I'd been quicker to think."

He flashed her a smile, and every time he did, it was more heart-melty than the last. "How do you do that?"

Should she tell him? No one currently in her life had any idea. Livy wrestled with the decision. It was in the past, but it had affected her entire life.

His warm hand wrapped around hers. "I will not let it leave my lips. No one will ever know."

She pulled her gaze from the cushion to his and nodded. It had been six days since meeting him, and never in her life would she have even considered telling anyone. Only, she trusted him more than she'd ever trusted anyone. He'd saved her life.

"My first foster home was great, but I knew it was temporary going in. They just took in kids while their social worker found them a more permanent place. It took them a while, and I was nine by the time a real foster home became available. My second placement didn't last long either, maybe a few months. I don't know what happened. I just remember a social worker picking me up after school and telling me that I'd be staying with a new family."

"Okay."

"My third placement was with Bret and Suzanne Nathanson. They had a teenage boy, Michael, who was thirteen. We got along okay, but he wasn't exactly thrilled to share his parents."

Gabe nodded, and she continued.

"Bret, my foster dad, loved me. For some reason, we just hit it off right away. When I was younger, before all the...I was different. I was outgoing, a little bit of a smart-mouth, headstrong. He loved all those things about me. I was also angry and hurt, but he'd sit with me after school while I did my homework, take me to the park, and let me cry, yell, and scream." Her chest tightened. She'd really liked him.

"That doesn't sound so bad."

"It wasn't until Michael decided he didn't want me there anymore. He hated that his dad was spending time with me. He started telling all kinds of lies about me. From breaking lamps, vases, and pictures to cutting up the couch and ransacking the house. His dad was a little hesitant to believe him, but his mom... she was on board from the moment it started."

Gabe nodded again.

"She would rip into me and call me all sorts of names. I'd beg her to believe me, and the look she gave me—I was the worst person on the planet. She never gave me the benefit of the doubt. I was the bad seed, and that's all there was to it." She wiped away a tear streaking down her cheek. Crying over what happened wasn't something she let herself do anymore.

"At that point, Suzanne wanted me gone too. I don't know if Bret believed all the lies or not, but he'd say I was just acting out because I lost my parents. That they needed to be understanding and give me a little time to come to terms with it. If they were in my shoes, how would they feel after having just lost everything they knew." She swiped another tear off her cheek. "That's kind of where I got the idea to understand people, because Bret tried to understand me. It made an impact and stayed with me."

"Okay."

"One night, Bret and Suzanne went to a party a few blocks over. Michael came into my room and told me to get up. That we needed to take a walk. I said no. He put his hand around my throat and choked me until I nearly passed out." She took a deep breath and let it out slowly. "He said that if I didn't get up, the next time he wouldn't stop squeezing until I was dead, so I did as he said."

"Livy."

"We lived in Belle Glade, Florida, maybe a mile or so from a sugarcane plantation. There I was, in a nightgown in the middle of summer, and the mosquitos were like locusts. I was being eaten alive, but I kept walking with Michael. He stopped at the edge of a field of sugarcane and told me to go into the cane field." This part of the story took her breath away and brought back memories that gave her nightmares.

Gabe gave her a pained look.

She forced tears back and continued on with the story. "I said no and tried to run back to the house. The next thing I knew, something hit me, and everything was fuzzy. I couldn't stand or speak. Michael picked me up, and everything went black. When I woke up, I had no idea where I was or how to get home. I had bites all over me and was terrified."

"How long were you out there?"

"It took a few days for searchers to find me, but by the time they did, I'd been labeled troubled. Michael told them I had been the one to lure him out into the field and that he'd run as soon as he could. He'd given himself bruises and cuts, and because of all the lies he'd been telling, everyone believed him."

"Even Bret?"

"Yeah. He said he'd tried to understand me and he'd never been so disappointed in someone in his whole life. He'd trusted me, and I'd broken that trust. He made me feel horrible. But I knew he was a good man. I saw and felt it."

"Didn't they know how Michael was at all? I mean, were there signs?"

She shook her head. "He was so good at manipulating people. It was something out of a movie. He just...he looked the part of a nice kid, but he was highly intelligent, and he just knew what to say to people."

"So, Bret and Suzanne didn't even question him?"

"No, and he was their son. I mean, I think it would be hard to believe the worst about your kid. A few years ago, I got curious and looked him up. He's currently in prison for a Ponzi scheme, which surprised me. I thought he might be in jail, but for killing someone."

"Wow."

Pausing, she sighed and shrugged. "I don't even think Suzanne was all that bad. I don't think she wanted to foster or adopt. I think Bret talked her into it, and she was taking her anger out on me. Now that I'm older, there are times I've felt trapped and haven't reacted well. We say we'll do one thing or another if something happens, but until it actually happens, we have no idea."

"How are you not jaded, though? After what Suzanne and Michael did? Wasn't it hard to see the good in them?"

She shrugged. "I was angry and bitter for a little bit, and then I realized the only person who was miserable was me. I slowly let it go, and I promised myself I'd try to understand people and find a reason behind their actions because it gave me peace. And as long as I'm happy and content, that's all that mattered to me."

"Why did you move around to so many foster homes, though?"

"My record said I'd tried to hurt someone's kid. Anytime there was a questionable event, all eyes fell on me, and it wasn't long before I was moved again. It didn't matter how hard I tried. No one wanted me."

He pulled her into a hug, and she melted into him. No one had ever held her as if they were afraid she was going to get away. "I will never let anyone hurt you again, and if they try, I'll crush them."

It was a nice sentiment, but she knew it was just that. Still, she appreciated the ferocity of his tone and the words. "I've never told anyone about that except Tori, and that was a few years after I knew her. Definitely not Jacob. Something always stopped me."

"You're safe with me." He rubbed his hands up and down her back with soothing strokes. "It will never leave my lips."

She'd never felt more secure. Another tear ran

down her cheek. Then another. Soon they were falling faster than she could catch them, and she sobbed.

Gabe pulled her closer, never saying a word, just letting her cry.

It was the kindest thing anyone had ever done for her. Letting her weep over her childhood.

CHAPTER 14

*G*abe watched Livy as she slept in his arms, marveling at her character. She had the right to be the most bitter person Gabe had ever met. After what she went through as a child, and then with Jacob, there would've been no faulting her. If she hadn't told him about the things that happened to her, he would have never guessed the extent of what happened. Not by the way she treated him.

Instead, she was the sweetest woman he'd ever come in contact with. Considerate, caring, funny, and intelligent were her personal trademark. Now that he knew about her past, he respected her ability to see the good in people even more.

He'd slammed a door in her face, and instead of being angry, she'd responded with understanding.

Even finding out he'd kept his identity from her, she was gracious and forgiving, not treating him any different.

It had been nothing to tell her about Rachelle. He was tea in a wide pitcher with as fast as he'd poured his heart out. She'd said nothing while he did it. He didn't realize how much he'd needed someone to just listen. Not to offer a solution or tell him to let it go.

Livy sighed, pressing her hand against his chest as she slept. He'd held her while she wept horrible heart-breaking cries until she couldn't cry another tear. When she'd tried to retreat to her room, he'd held on to her. She may have thought it was for her, but it wasn't.

Never had he felt such a strong desire to protect and shield someone. When he said he'd never let anyone hurt her ever again, he'd meant it. Even if they only remained friends, he'd make sure no one ever said another unkind thing to her or put their hands on her again. He didn't care what he had to do to keep his word either.

Livy stirred, and her eyes opened. She blinked a few times until her eyes focused. "Oh no, I fell asleep on you."

When she tried to break away, he shook his head and said, "I don't mind at all." He rubbed his thumb along her cheek. The dark circles around her eyes were getting lighter, and he intended to see them gone.

"How long have I been asleep?"

"A few hours."

Worry lines creased her forehead, and she touched her fingers to her lips. "I'm sorry. I kinda fell apart."

He pressed his lips to her forehead and held it a moment. "You can fall apart on me anytime." When he pulled back, her eyes were wide.

"You kissed my forehead."

"Yes, I did." It took restraint to *just* do that. He wanted to kiss her soft lips. "I care about you and wanted to show you, and you deserve to be cared about. And I don't want you to question whether or not I did it because I felt sorry for you or that I was being nice or any of the other multitude of reasons you could come up with. I know how you struggle with your worth and explaining things away, and I want you to know it was because I wanted to and no other reason."

Her eyes grew wider. "Gabe, I—"

"No."

"But—"

"No. Whatever excuse or reason you're thinking for why I shouldn't want to kiss you, just forget it.

Unless you just hate my guts, I'll continue to show you I care, and I'll mean every bit of it. I can promise you that." And by kiss, he meant a lot more than on the forehead.

Her lips parted, and his willpower was stretched to its limit. For a heartbeat, she stared at him, her cheeks blanketed pink. "I don't hate your guts."

He smiled. "Good, because I don't know when those snowplows will be here, and I'd hate to be sharing a cabin with someone who despised me."

"I should probably work on my book."

"It's the middle of the night. Aren't you tired?"

With a small nod, she looked down and said, "Yeah, I am, but I don't know if I can go to sleep."

"How about a midnight snack and something to drink, and I'll get the fire going again?"

She shrugged. "I'll get sleepy, but I doubt I'll be able to sleep."

"We'll figure that out when the time comes."

"Okay."

Gabe held Livy as he stood and set her feet on the floor. "I really am glad you're here."

Staring up at him, her little pink lips parted as if the words were foreign to her.

"Would you get the snacks and drinks?" he asked. "I'll get the fire started."

Livy's cheeks turned bright pink, and she nodded. "Sure."

He smiled and left the living room as she headed to the kitchen. Ten minutes later, they were spread out on her thick pallet of blankets, snacking on a plate of fruit and watching the fire.

"These strawberries are really good. I didn't expect them to be so sweet. Not here in Montana," Livy said.

"I didn't either, but they sure are." Suddenly, he was even more aware of her lips and wondered how they'd taste with the added sweetness of strawberries. If he didn't stop, he was going to kiss her, and he couldn't. Not when he didn't know how she felt about him yet. So far, he had been the one chasing her.

She finished the one she was nibbling on and lay down on her back. "I think I'm good."

"Full or just really tired?"

"Yes." She smiled and closed her eyes, laying her hand over her stomach.

He slid the plate from between them and closed a bit of the distance. "Think you'll be able to sleep?"

"No, but I'm comfortable."

Closing the rest of the gap between them, he propped himself on his elbow and put his head in his hand. "It isn't just because you worry that you can't sleep?"

She opened her eyes and shook her head. "Most of the time, I have horrible nightmares, and I just don't like to sleep. I'm scared of the dark."

"Because of Michael?"

"Yeah," she whispered. "Him, and when I woke up, I was covered in bugs and could hear wild pigs everywhere. I'd never been so scared."

Her face was pointed at him, and he couldn't resist brushing his fingertips across her cheek. "You're safe here. If anyone tries to hurt you, they'll be going through me." He took her by the waist and tugged her to him until her shoulder was pressed against his chest. "I won't let anything happen to you."

"I don't know why, but I believe you."

He combed his fingers through her hair, and her eyes slid shut. The longer he combed her hair, the more she relaxed she became until she was breathing evenly.

With a soft sigh, she rolled into him, and he curled his body around her. Man, he loved the feel of her body next to his. He liked the peace he felt when he was with her. She was a balm to him. He'd felt so bruised and cut when he'd arrived, and now the wounds were healing and the bruises were fading. He wondered if he was doing the same for her.

LIVY TOOK in a lungful of air and ran her hand along the arm holding her. Slowly, she opened her eyes and looked down. Gabe. Her back was molded to his body, and his muscular arm was pinning her to him. A tingling sensation started at the tip of her head and traveled down to her toes.

"Did you sleep well?" he asked.

He loosened his hold just enough that she could turn and face him, and then he tightened it again. It was the best jail she'd ever been in. She'd slept fantastically. "I can't remember ever waking up so rested."

His smile made her heart stutter. "Good. Your dark circles are getting better too, and your eyes are brighter."

She didn't know what to think or say. He'd held her all night long. Jacob had never even done that. Knowing Jacob was with her, even if it was just in spirit, had helped her, but he'd always been out late partying or gone to surfing competitions.

Gabe had kissed her forehead. It had been sweet and innocent and intimate all at once. He'd said he cared about her and he was sealing it with a kiss. He'd promised her his affection was sincere and that he'd continue to show it. Her pulse jumped at what that might mean.

"I have an idea," Gabe said.

"What?"

"Let's get dressed as warm as we can and go play in the snow. It's been a long time since I've done that, and it sounds fun."

She laughed. "I don't know if I've ever played in the snow."

"Well, then, this is the perfect time." His eyes twinkled with mischief, and she wondered just what he had planned.

"Okay."

He shot her a hair-melting smile and stood, pulling her with him. "Meet you at the front door in ten."

"I can beat that."

"You're on!" He bolted from the living room toward his room.

"That's cheating!" She scrambled after him and ran to her room. There was no way she could let him win. After digging in her suitcase, she dressed in a pair of jeans, layered two t-shirts with a sweater, and dashed out of her room, to find Gabe leaned against the front door, looking like an outdoors magazine model. "You totally cheated."

"I did not. I won fair and square."

Her mouth dropped open. "You did not. You totally got a head start."

One corner of his mouth twitched up. "I didn't. You said you could beat that. I took it as the starting bell."

"Fine," she said and pulled on her boots and coat.

When she finished, he opened the door for her and followed her out, letting it shut behind them. For a second, she tensed. The last time she'd gone outside, she'd nearly frozen to death.

"It's unlocked." He winked, seeming to read her mind.

"Guess I'm a little antsy."

He took her chin in his fingers and tipped her face up. His dark eyes locked with hers, and the intensity with which he looked at her made her stomach flutter. "With every reason to be. I gave you my word that I'd never let anything happen to you again. I meant it."

Her knees wobbled slightly. If he didn't stop that sultry gaze, she'd be done for. It also reminded her of his kiss on her forehead and his promise that he truly cared and would continue to show it, and that made it even harder to stand. Her brain was so mushy at the moment that the best she'd be able to do was to squeak, so she just nodded.

Gabe stood there a heartbeat, his gaze roaming

from her eyes to her lips and back like he was tempted to kiss her right then and there. For the life of her, she couldn't picture an excuse for him kissing her that would be anything other than simply wanting to. And, boy, did she want him to want to. But it had to be her imagination. The close quarters were playing with her head.

"Let's see what trouble we can find." He stopped at the edge of the porch. "I wonder how deep this snow is." Holding onto the stair railing, Gabe stepped off and sank into the snow up to his waist. Laughing, he looked over his shoulder. "I'm not sure this is safe for you. Will you be able to see over the snow?"

Livy scoffed, but she couldn't stop the smile from spreading on her lips. "That's not funny. I'm not that short!"

"There are Oompa Loompas taller than you." He threw his head back and laughed.

"You take that back!" Livy dashed to the edge of the porched, scooped up a handful of snow, and lobbed a snowball at him, smacking him square in the cheek.

It stunned him long enough that he just stared at her before balling up a handful of snow and retaliating. She dodged the snowball and formed another, hitting him again.

"I might be short, but I have better aim." She stuck her tongue out at him.

"Oh, you are so going down." He climbed out of the snow, formed a ball with the powder, and let it fly.

They traded throw after throw for who knows how long, with Gabe missing her each time until the last. He hit her dead center in the stomach and knocked her on her butt. She landed with an *oomph* and glared at him.

He threw his head back and laughed so hard he had to wipe his eyes. "That makes up for all the times I missed."

Livy stood and narrowed her eyes. He was definitely getting it.

His eyes went wide as she charged forward, lunged off the porch, and tackled him. They crashed backward into the snow and rolled, with him landing on top of her.

She knew the moment he looked at her that she was in trouble. His fingers found her waist, and he began tickling her. She barked with laughter and squealed as she tried to get away, but the harder she tried, the harder he held on.

"Stop! Stop! Truce!" she yelled.

"Truce?"

Laughing so hard she couldn't speak, she nodded and managed to get out, "Yes."

"I told you that you were going down," he said as he held her gaze.

Livy grabbed his hat and pulled it over his eyes, and he yanked it off, causing his hair to stick out at funny angles. She burst out laughing again.

He shook his head and pulled his hat back onto his head and down over his ears. "I'm starting to freeze." Then he yanked her hat down over her eyes.

A piece of her hair fell on her lips, and she blew it off before pulling her hat up enough that she could see. His laughter had stopped, and he was looking at her with an unreadable expression.

"This was fun," she said.

"Yeah, it was." A small smile reappeared on his lips. "Thanks for agreeing to play in the snow with me."

With him looking at her like that, she'd play in the snow—or anything else he wanted to do—until her fingers fell off. He smelled so good. She loved how safe she felt when he was holding her. Her heart singsonged, *You're falling for him.*

It terrified her. She'd loved once, and it had nearly broken her. Jacob would say the words, but his actions would scream the opposite. Could she trust herself enough to believe that someone could care about her? Someone good like Gabe?

"Are you ready to sit by the fire and thaw out?" he asked.

"Yeah. I'm freezing."

Gabe stood and helped her up. "I think I'm going to take a hot shower first," he said as he stomped snow off his shoes at the front door.

"That's a good idea."

"See you at the fireplace in thirty?"

She smiled. "I'll let you win this one." She winked, tossed her boots, and ran for her room. It would take longer than thirty minutes to get herself warm and her thoughts under control. If she could. The longer she stayed at the cabin, the harder it was getting.

CHAPTER 15

Gabe scrubbed his face with his hands as hot water sluiced over him. It felt as though his core was made of solid ice, but it was worth it. Livy's laughter had filled the air, and it was a melody he couldn't get enough of. Her smile and the way her eyes sparkled was worth every snowball hit.

Then she'd tackled him, and it had taken every ounce of strength he had not to crush his lips to hers. The only thing that saved him was the fact that he actually *was* freezing. And he knew if he was, she was too.

His phone began ringing, so he turned the water off, threw a towel around his waist, and left a trail of water on the way to the nightstand. With a swipe of his finger, he answered his mom's call. "Hello?"

"Well, don't you sound cheery." Her tone said he needed to explain.

"I'm in a better mood."

"I see. Does it have anything to do with our cabin guest?"

Gabe grinned. Should he talk to his mom about her? "I enjoy spending time with her."

He could see his mom's smile spreading on her face. "Oh?"

"She's different."

"Well, then maybe she'd agree to attend the dinner party I'm throwing when you get back."

His eyebrows knitted together. "Dinner party?"

"I thought it would be nice to invite Romero Publishing's authors to a party. It's a good way to introduce ourselves without seeming…"

"Intimidating?"

"Yes, that's the word. We invite Saxon authors, and they can rub elbows, soften any preconceived notions."

"Before or after we make the announcement?"

His mom inhaled slowly. In his mind, she was rubbing the platinum heart necklace his father had given her between her fingers. "I was thinking we'd do it at the party."

Gabe considered it a moment. "I like that. We're

making the announcement, but we're letting them hear it first. It makes us look good."

"Exactly what I was thinking."

"That's good."

"You think Ms. Weber will come?"

He smiled. His mom sure enjoyed meddling. "I want her to."

"Care to talk about it?"

"Not yet. I don't know what to say yet."

"Gabe?"

Water pooled at his feet, and he was getting chilly from standing there in a towel. "Yeah?"

"Is she anything like Rachelle?"

"Not even close. Rachelle couldn't touch the soles of her shoes."

He felt the beam of his mom's smile through the phone. "I like her already, then."

"I need to get dressed. She's waiting for me in the living room."

"Okay, love. Talk to you soon."

"Bye, Mom."

Gabe dried off and dressed in a pair of sweatpants and a t-shirt, hoping Livy was already out there. He was a schoolboy with a deadly crush. Being with her made him feel light and happy. And anytime she wasn't near, he felt her absence. He just wished he knew how she felt about him. They'd only known each other for a week.

As he opened his door, Livy opened hers and stepped out. A light floral scent floated from her and took him by the nose, drawing him closer.

She smiled as he neared. "Guess we're both slow, huh?"

"I got a call from my mom."

Her smile fell. "Is everything okay?"

"Yeah, she just had an idea and wanted to run it past me."

"Oh. Good."

She started to take a step, and Gabe stopped her. "We're going to throw a dinner party when I get back and invite all of Romero Publishing's authors to it. We're going to make the announcement there."

Her eyes widened. "Oh. Wow. That's quick."

"As soon as I get home, the deal's done."

She nodded as her thumb came to her lips and she chewed on it.

"I want you to come. With me. As my date."

Her head slowly lifted, and her eyes locked with his. "Oh."

"Would you?"

She tilted her head and blinked. "You'd want me? But all those people in your circle…"

"Don't mean anything to me, and you are just as valuable. More so." His heart was beating so hard he could swear she could hear it too. "I want to take you."

Her lashes fanned against her cheeks as she looked down, and his heart began to slide to the floor. "But a party? Wouldn't you want to take someone...used to those kinds of things? Someone better suited than me?"

With one finger he tipped her chin up. "I know I'm asking for something that's outside of your comfort zone. I know it's a lot to consider, but there is no one else I want to take. You're intelligent, witty, interesting, and beautiful." He smiled. "Selfishly, I'm thinking if I show up with you on my arm, it'll make me look better."

Her cheeks turned bright pink as she held his gaze. Her face was a complete mask, and he was terrified she'd say no. Maybe she wasn't feeling the same about him as he was her. It was all he could do not to brace his hand against the wall and hold his breath.

Slowly, she nodded, and a smile twitched on her lips. "I'd really like to go with you."

"You will?" The question rushed out as an exhale. It was a fist-pump-in-the-air type of moment. He was elated.

She nodded. "As long as I get to spend time with you."

It was the best thing he'd heard in a long time. "Good."

He could barely refrain from kissing her, but if he kissed her right now, she'd say it was because he wanted her to be his date. When was he ever going to get to kiss her and not have to worry about her finding an excuse? How could he get her to understand that the people who had assigned her value were wrong?

"You are so beautiful."

Her lashes fanned out against her cheeks again as she lowered her gaze. She had to know how beautiful she was.

He tipped her chin with his finger. "You are. I've thought that since the moment I met you. Getting to know you has only enhanced your beauty."

A smile spread on her lips, sending a crushing rush of temptation through him, and a small giggle popped out. "You're very sweet."

"Honesty is another of my attributes, despite what you might think. I felt bad about not being honest in the beginning, but..." Now it was his turn to lower his gaze. He felt ashamed.

Livy leaned in and caught his gaze. "I don't doubt your honesty or your sincerity."

He cleared his throat. Her lips were screaming to be kissed. If only their stomachs weren't growling for food. They sounded like a choir, and both of them erupted into laughter.

He placed a hand on his stomach. "I just realized we haven't eaten all day."

"Me too. Share a sandwich?"

"How about pancakes?"

Her eyes widened. "Oh yeah. With bacon?"

"I'll make the pancakes if you make the bacon."

"Deal."

GABE STRETCHED his legs out in front of him and leaned back on his elbows. His stomach was full, and now he was drowsy. Working with Livy in the kitchen was more a dance than actual work. It had been as much fun as the snowball fight.

She was stretched out next to him, her hand draped across her stomach with her head turned in his direction. "I'll never eat again."

With a chuckle, he rolled onto his side and

propped himself on his elbow with his head resting in his hand. "Yeah, I think I overate."

"It's hard to put the shovel down when it's pancakes and bacon."

His body shook as he laughed. She was the only person since Rachelle to make him laugh like that. "True."

She smiled wide. "My stomach's complaining, but I'm not."

"I haven't had this much fun in a long time. I never thought I'd be thankful for a snowstorm."

Livy caught her bottom lip in her teeth. "Me neither."

With a slight shrug, he asked, "Which part?"

"Both."

"You're not worried anymore?"

Her smile faded, and her gaze held his. "A little, but each day seems to be better."

"Can I tell you something?"

"Always," she said softly.

"I talked to Rachelle."

"You did?"

He nodded, touching his cut with his fingertips. The cut wasn't pretty, but it didn't require a bandage anymore. "That night I hit my head."

Livy's gaze traveled to his forehead and back down to his eyes. "So that's what woke you up."

"Yeah, she didn't care that it was late or that I was sleeping."

"What did she say?"

Gabe chuckled. It seemed absurd now. "She wanted to check on me. Her way of trying to get back together."

"Oh."

"I told her it was over and to not call me again. Then I hung up on her."

Livy rolled onto her side, and her eyes went wide. "You did?"

"I've never done that so boldly before. There was always a part of me that hoped she'd change, but I realized she wasn't going to. I was finally done waiting for something that was never going to happen."

"It's easy and hard at the same time. Telling Jacob I was done was liberating and terrifying all at once. A small part of me wondered if his scraps were better than nothing. Then I thought, 'I'd rather have nothing than whatever it was I was getting from him.'"

She sure had a way with words. No wonder she was an author. "Exactly. Knowing Rachelle, though, I'll need to say it a few more times before she gets it."

"I'll have to change my number again. I'm tired of

dealing with Jacob. More than likely, he'll show up at my door again when I get home."

Gabe's jaw clenched. "Have you thought about taking out a restraining order on him?"

"Oh, no, he's harmless, just a pest. He doesn't love me." She covered her mouth with her hand as she yawned. "I don't even know why he keeps coming back."

"Getting sleepy?"

"A full stomach and warmth will do that." She laughed. "Plus, I think I could sleep a year and still need a nap."

Gabe rolled onto his back with his arm behind his head as he kept his gaze trained on her. Had he been pushing himself on her? He'd initiated most of their interactions. It was easy to get caught up in wanting to help someone and have it cross a line.

Next thing he knew, she closed the distance and lay next to him. "Are you okay?"

He flattened his hand against the small of her back and pulled her closer. "I'm fine now."

"Why did you look so sad, then?"

"I thought I was pushing myself on you, and I don't want to do that."

His breath caught as she trailed her fingertips along his jaw and curled her hand around the back of his neck. She held his gaze and said, "You aren't. I've spent my life not being wanted. It's hard to shift gears when someone comes along and starts challenging everything you've ever thought about yourself. It's not something that changes overnight."

"I think I understand that. I've been working so hard for the last year that it's been almost impossible for me to shift gears. It's why I was glad you were here."

"Why were you working so hard?"

Should he tell her that too? He'd already told her more than anyone else. "After Rachelle left me, I found her in Cape Cod with another man. She was livid that I'd chased her to his home, but I just wanted to know why she did it."

Livy put her fingers to her lips but stayed quiet. Man, he appreciated that about her.

It was hard to breathe. As far as he knew, no one knew what she'd said to him that day. "She flung words like they were knives. The man she was with was better than me. I was worthless. She said my dad had wished he could've been proud of me, but he'd never been so disappointed in one of his children."

Her mouth dropped open with a tiny gasp, and her eyebrows knitted together.

"My dad and I had argued about the direction my

life was going right before he died. I wasn't living up to my potential, but I didn't want to work my life away. I wanted to have balance. I wanted a family. I didn't care about money the way he did.

"It wasn't long after that argument that I lost him, and we still hadn't worked everything out. She knew how guilty I felt, and it just cut me to pieces. After that, I threw everything I was into Saxon Publishing. It was going to be the most successful publishing company in New York, even if it killed me."

Her fingers wrapped around his hand and squeezed.

"I was working all the time. I didn't care. I started having headaches. I'd go days without eating. My mom and siblings would make me stop and eat. I wasn't sleeping well. Not chronic like yours, but not well-rested, for sure. The headaches turned into migraines. They'd hit without warning, and they were crippling.

"About two months ago, I collapsed during a meeting. My family tried to get me to take a break then, but I refused. We had a deal in the works, and this company was only willing to deal with me. I had no excuse this time, though. I was either taking a break willingly or by force."

"You collapsed?"

He nodded. "My mom didn't know it, but I was on the verge of it happening again before I came here. That night I got here, I was kind of a mess."

She touched the side of his face, and her eyes glistened. "I won't ever let that happen again."

There was something about the way she said it that made his heart beat a little faster. "It's hard to take care of yourself when you don't think you're worth it."

"You're worth a whole lot." There was a tiny pause. "To me." She laid her head on his chest and stretched her arm across his waist. "A whole lot."

He'd never shared Rachelle's words with anyone. Before now, the thought would have made him sick to his stomach, but telling Livy was the right thing to do. It was out, and another weight had been thrown off. The more time he spent at the cabin with her, the lighter he felt. And she had come to him tonight. Maybe this thing wasn't one-sided after all.

CHAPTER 16

*L*ivy and Gabe stood in the doorway as they watched snowplows pass in front of the cabin.

The noisy trucks had jolted them awake just moments earlier.

He was curled around her with his arms around her waist. She felt so safe when he was holding her. He was her concrete bunker. There was no way anyone or anything was getting to her as long as she was in his arms.

When he'd pulled away the night before, she'd closed the gap without a second thought. It was a new move for her. She never would've done that before, but she liked his warmth and how she felt when she was next to him. Being held by him, waking up in his arms, it was something she could easily get used to. He was afraid he was pushing himself on her? What would he think if he knew she couldn't get enough of him?

"You aren't leaving, right?" For a second, he sounded as disappointed as she felt to see the snow cleared off the road.

He'd asked her to a company party as his date. Or was it a date? Could he really be interested in her? Maybe he was just being nice and since she was an author with Romero publishing, it was a way to get her there. She was their most successful author. But Gabe wasn't like that. He wouldn't treat her like that. Still, that didn't mean it was a date. It was just two people who were required to be at the same function showing up together. They were stranded together, after all. At least she had a few days to psych herself up for it.

Just as well to get that notion out of her head. As soon as they left the cabin, their popsicle-stick world would crumble. He was a billionaire. She didn't even know what to think about that. Talk about different worlds. She had nothing growing up. What must it be like to have everything? Did she even want to know? Sure, she had a good income, but she didn't keep most of it.

After spending years in the foster system being bounced around, she liked the idea of giving back to kids at the local orphanage because she personally knew the people and they loved the kids in the home. It wasn't the most ideal situation, to have no parents, but every kid needed to be loved, and she could only imagine if someone had loved her how different her opinion of herself would be.

What would meeting Gabe's family be like? Were they normal, or would she be disappointed in how Gabe and his family threw around money? Would it change the way she saw him or the way he treated her? Her heart sank at the possibility.

Plus, she was now an author in his publishing company. If her career went south, what would that do to them? Like there was a "them." What an unbelievably ridiculous thought. They were friends, and most likely they were friends because he had no other choice. He'd probably only invited her to go with him because he felt sorry for her and he didn't want to go alone.

That didn't mean she wanted the dream to fade just yet. "Not if you don't want me to."

He squeezed her tighter. "I don't want you to." He released her, and she shut the door.

She smiled and leaned her back against it. "I don't hear any snowplows, do you?"

"Not anymore." He rubbed his thumbs under her eyes. "Almost gone."

"Thank you. I know that big pile of blankets isn't as comfortable as a bed."

"I feel great." His eyes narrowed. "And no, I'm not just saying that."

"I wasn't thinking that."

He lifted one eyebrow.

She rolled her eyes. "Okay, maybe a little."

He'd told her something so deep and personal the night before that she almost couldn't believe it was real. How could he ever think he wasn't good enough? He'd been kind to her. It had been nearly impossible not to kiss him. He'd looked so sad and vulnerable. That anyone would say anything so hateful and cruel to him blew her mind.

"Want to get a shower, make some breakfast, and then see what trouble we can get into today?" he asked.

"I believe Saxon Publishing is wanting a book from me. I have twenty percent left, and I know where I'm going. I think there's a good chance I could finish it in the next couple of days."

Gabe narrowed his eyes. "Wow. You really are fast."

"I hope Tori likes it. I sent her the first half of the book."

"Can I read it when you finish?"

The corners of her mouth twitched up. She couldn't believe he wanted to read it. "No."

"Please?"

"Maybe."

He slapped a hand over his heart. "Ouch, you know how to cut a guy."

"You're so silly."

"I need that shower and some breakfast. How about you?"

She nodded. "Yeah, but can you beat me?" She pushed off of him and raced to her room where she stripped as she ran to the bathroom. There was no way he was going to beat her this time. Fourteen minutes and thirty-three seconds later, she was showered, dressed, and walking into the kitchen.

Gabe shot her a smile as he leaned back from the open door of the fridge. "I can beat you." He'd worn jeans and a t-shirt too. Only he looked better in his. He could fill out a pair of jeans like no one's business.

"I have a lot more hair to wash."

"Yeah, but I'm taller. I have a lot more skin to wash."

Livy felt the blood rush to her cheeks. She did not

need to be thinking about his skin or how much he had to wash. As she walked to him, he held out a strawberry, and she plucked it from his hand. "Man, these are so good." As she bit into it, juice ran down her chin, and she held her hand under it as she rushed to the sink. "And juicy too."

She finished the strawberry as she wiped the juice off of her. When she turned around, Gabe was staring at her. "What?"

He crossed the two feet separating them, picked her up, and set her on the counter. "Remember that promise?"

"Yeah," she whispered as her racing heart ticked up three notches.

He took her face in his hands, and for a heartbeat, he held her gaze before pressing his lips to hers.

The feel of him was like nothing she could have expected. Warm tingles spread from her lips down into the pit of her stomach. She ran her hands up his muscled chest, around his neck, and threaded her fingers in the silkiest head of hair she'd ever touched.

His hands left her face and traveled to her shoulders where they stayed just a second before roaming down her back as he pulled her to him in an embrace that left no room for space between them. When he deepened the kiss, a groan came from so deep in his throat that she felt his chest rumble.

Kissing him…oh, kissing him made her soul sing. There wasn't a scene she'd written that could top the flutter of butterflies in her stomach or how the feel of his hard masculine body against hers made her want to forget the world existed.

He cupped the back of her head with his hand and continued kissing her like he was making up for time he'd lost. Never in her life had she enjoyed being kissed by someone as much as she enjoyed kissing him. She was sure her very essence depended on him continuing to kiss her. When his lips left hers, he trailed light kisses across her cheek, down her jawline, and stopped at the hollow of her throat.

She was sure she was low on oxygen, and she didn't care. All she wanted was his lips back on hers. It was though a cold wind had hit them, and she needed him to bring warmth back to them.

He found his way back and kissed her again, exploring her mouth while she explored his.

When they finally pulled back for air, it was like all the sunshine had been taken away. He touched his forehead to hers as he tried to catch his breath. "I want you to hear me. I kissed you because I wanted to. I kissed you because I couldn't fathom your lips not tasting as sweet as I imagined them. I kissed you because I didn't have the strength to not kiss you anymore."

Her lungs burned, and her breathing was ragged. She slid her hands down his back, enjoying the way the muscles felt beneath her hands. "I hear you."

Touching her lips to his, it ignited another toe-curling kiss from him. Bracing one hand on the counter, he pressed his body harder against hers while he flattened his other hand against her back.

Just when she thought she'd have to beg for air, he broke the kiss, and she immediately regretted even thinking it. Air was overrated.

No one had ever kissed her like that. No one. He set her blood on fire. His kiss had given her a glimpse of what she should expect from a passionate kiss, and she couldn't imagine ever going back to the fireless kisses she'd experienced before. Gabe had awakened something in her, and mediocre was no longer good enough.

Even when this bubble burst—which it would as soon as he saw how ill-fit she was for his world of posh homes, fancy parties, and sophisticated people —she wasn't making excuses for people anymore. Or, she was at least going to try. It might take some time, but he'd given her something she'd not had before. Courage and enough confidence to expect more.

GABE STARED at Livy as she sat on the couch with her computer in her lap. Her puffy, kiss-bruised lips were begging for more attention from him. He could have kissed her all day and never been satisfied. There was no way he'd ever feel with another woman what he felt when he was kissing her. His body ached to be near her, but they'd had to break apart because she wasn't getting any work done, and his lungs were too air-deprived to stay next to her.

"You have to be close to done," he said.

She smiled as she glanced at him. "Patience."

"How much?"

"Patience."

"I swear if you call me grasshopper, I'm chucking that laptop and kissing you until you beg for mercy."

A smile spread on her lips. "You'd be surprised how little mercy I need."

Gabe pinched his lips together. She had no idea how tempted he was to toss that computer. "Livy."

"Read. I'll be done in a little bit."

He raked his hand through his hair and returned

his attention to the book he was reading. Of course, it was one of hers. It was just as good as the last, too.

On the cushion next to her, her phone rang. She answered it and stared at the screen. "Hey, Tori."

"I need the rest of that book. You can't leave me hanging. That's just cruel, Liv."

Livy giggled. "Hey, you're the one who said to send you what I had."

Gabe needed them to stop talking. She was never going to finish, and it was killing him. "And she'll never get it to you if don't let her work."

"Let me see him," Tori said.

Gabe switched seats, and Tori came into view. "You want the last pages, right?"

"Have you read it?" she asked.

"No, she won't let me."

Tori looked at Livy. "He wants to read it?"

"I've read one of her books, and I'm halfway through another."

Tori's mouth dropped open, and her gaze darted from Livy to him. "I was right, wasn't I?"

"Right about what?" asked Livy.

"Nothing," they both said at the same time.

Livy narrowed her eyes and leaned back to look at Gabe. "Right. I think I'm going to type a little slower."

Gabe growled and changed seats again. He would

wait until she was off the phone, and then he'd see just how strong her resolve was.

Tori laughed. "So, Saxon is having a dinner party. Romero authors and employees are invited. I know you hate these things, but I needed to tell you."

Livy darted her gaze to Gabe. "Yeah, I think I'll be at this one."

"What? Who are you? Have you been body-snatched?"

"No, I just want to go."

Gabe changed seats again. "My name is Gabriel Saxon, and she'll be coming with me."

Tori's eyes grew so large that he thought they were going to pop out. "You're…"

"Yes."

"And she's…"

"Yep."

Tori's lips spread into a wide smile. "Well, then you'd better get yourselves here. It's in less than a week, and it's black tie. You need a dress, my little jeans-and-pajamas darling."

Livy's face fell. "Black tie? I'll never be able to find a dress."

"Yes, you will," Gabe said as he stood and walked into the kitchen. He pulled out his phone and called several of the designers he knew. By the time they got to the city, Livy would have her pick of whatever she wanted.

Then he called his mom. "Hey, Mom." He leaned his hip against the bar as he kept his eyes on Livy as she spoke to Tori.

"Hey, love."

"When did you schedule the party? Livy's agent just told us it's to be in a few days. I thought you wanted me here until I was ready to come home."

"I do, but Romero is pushing to give the announcement. If you aren't ready, I'll just tell them not yet."

"No, if they're pushing, we need to make the announcement."

"*Are* you ready to come home?"

He had to admit he was, but only if Livy was with him. "I don't know."

"You really like her, huh?"

"Yeah."

"Bring her home. I want to meet her. Brenden and Peter will both be in town. I'm sure Kath will want to meet her too."

Gabe rubbed his mouth with his hand. "They need to be gentle. She's been through a lot. Mom, I care about her. It goes deeper than anything I ever felt for Rachelle."

"What are you saying?"

"I don't know, but I need assurance that you'll help me keep her safe. She's not fragile, but she's sweet. If anyone hurts her, they'll see a darker side of my personality. I don't care if they're related or not."

His mom was quiet a moment. "Sounds like love, Gabe."

He cast his gaze to the floor. "I don't know what it is yet. Just promise me."

"Okay. I promise. We'll show her what a Saxon family wall looks like."

"Thanks."

"When will you be home?"

He looked up, and Livy locked eyes with him. "As soon as I can talk her into leaving."

"Okay. Bye, love."

"Bye, Mom."

He walked to the couch and sat beside her. She'd finished talking to Tori. "How's the book?"

"Just a little wrapping up to do, and I'll be done." She saved her document and closed down her computer. "I don't know about this party. I wasn't kidding when I said I was a wallflower."

Gabe took her hand and pressed it to his chest. "I'll be there the whole time." He pulled her onto his lap and kissed her. "Would you be horribly disappointed to go to New York? Like, leave now?"

Her eyes widened. "Now?"

"You need a dress, and I want to show you around New York City. What do you say?"

She held his gaze, seeming to debate something. "Are you sure you want to take me back to New York? It is a lot different there than here."

He held her tighter. "I'm absolutely positive. The only thing that will change is the scenery."

She lifted one cute little eyebrow. "Will you let me work on my book?"

If she was going to have to do that, then he was going to need a few of her kisses to tide him over. He cupped her cheek and pressed his lips to hers. The strawberry had worn off, but they were no less sweet.

She circled her arms around his neck and moaned as he deepened the kiss. He loved the feel of her lips against his. The softness of them. It was as if they were specifically made for him to kiss.

He pulled away, and she brushed those sweet, soft lips across his neck.

"We need to get packed," he said. His voice was low, and he could barely think.

"I'd rather kiss you."

"You have a book to finish."

She exhaled sharply and straightened. "Fine. I'll get packed. Then I'll show you just how fast I can type."

He smiled. "Looking forward to it."

Man, a few more of her kisses, and he'd be wrapped around her finger. Who was he kidding? He already was. He was also pretty sure he'd fallen for her.

CHAPTER 17

*I*t was after six in the evening when they landed in New York, and a limo had picked Livy and Gabe up. She'd ridden with him to the airport in his SUV to Sidney, Montana, when her car wouldn't start. Her Thing had always been temperamental, and she suspected it was mad she'd left it in the snow so long. Gabe had promised her he'd get someone to take care of it and that she'd find it in her driveway in Orlando when she got home.

The car pulled into a garage and parked in a spot nearest an elevator labeled private. "You have a private elevator?" Livy asked.

He smiled and nodded. "One of the perks of living on the top floor."

"Oh." The entire trip to New York had been spent with her trying to finish her book and picturing where Gabe lived.

It was one thing to wonder what his world was like. It was another to be walking around in it. As much as he'd assured her that he wanted her there, she was fighting the urge to flee. The only reason she'd agreed to come with him in the first place was because of his big brown eyes and that sizzling smile. Who in their right mind could turn him down?

She'd been disappointed to lose the last six days of her time in the cabin with him, but she figured if they'd spent that much time together, she never would've gotten over him after they went their separate ways. And this gave her the opportunity to see what he was like in the real world.

They got out of the car, grabbed their luggage, and stopped at the elevator. He pressed his thumb to a pad, and the doors opened. They stepped on, and the moment the doors shut, Gabe picked her up and pressed her against the wall.

"I'm so glad you're done with the book," he said. Then his lips were on hers, and she didn't care if she was done with the book or not.

Nothing existed but Gabe and the way he made her

feel. She wrapped her legs around his waist and buried her hands in his hair. His kisses were hard and demanding, like he'd waited years and not minutes since the last time he'd kissed her.

When the elevator doors opened, he groaned as they broke apart. "That ride wasn't nearly as long as it used to be," he said as he set her down.

He grabbed their luggage and pulled it behind him as they entered the most luxurious space she'd ever seen. Floor-to-ceiling windows lined the entire back wall, allowing a panoramic view of the city. "Wow." It was the most incredible view. Lights blinking and twinkling as far as she could see.

"You like it?"

"It's amazing. I can see why you picked it." She pulled her gaze from the view and took in the rest of his home.

The kitchen was to the left, and it was twice the size of the one in the cabin, with an island the size of a farm table in the middle. Dark wood cabinets with brushed nickel pulls lined the top and bottom of the walls. A formal dining room with a table that sat no less than twenty people was close enough that access was easy.

In the living room, there were two seating areas.

One was closer to the kitchen, meant for entertaining, and one was closer to a fireplace that sat to the right. The panoramic view could be seen as you lounged in front of it. It didn't feel cold at all, even with the tall ceilings, because of the warm brown painted walls. The posh atmosphere was overwhelming, and the looming feeling that maybe she was out of her element burned in the pit of her stomach.

"I'm glad you like it. Come on. I'll show you to your room."

Livy walked next to Gabe as he pulled her luggage behind him. They turned down a hall and entered a room halfway down. "Wow."

"I thought you might enjoy the view. I had Donna get the room ready while we were flying over."

"Donna?"

"My housekeeper. Although, I was hardly here the past year. Most of the time, I lived in my office. She was pretty happy to have something to do."

She tilted her head. "You kept her even though you didn't need her?"

"She's a single mom. Her little girl has autism and goes to a special school. It's important that she continues to attend. Plus, she's a great housekeeper, and I didn't want to lose her."

Just when Livy didn't think he could get any better.

This was the man kissing her on countertops and in elevators, holding her when she slept and promising to protect her. Rachelle was definitely an idiot for giving this up.

"My room is next door. No one can get in here without verification. You're absolutely safe here. Okay?"

She nodded. "Okay."

"I'm starved. Are you? I'm sure Donna stocked the fridge, but I'd rather go out."

"Sure."

He smiled. "Let me put my luggage up. I think I know a place you'll love."

She watched him leave with conflicting feelings. It was so easy to get caught up in his smile and his easy ways. The time she'd spent with him at the cabin made her comfortable with him. She was too quick to forget that this wasn't Montana. It was New York. Was he Gabe here? Or was he Gabriel Saxon, CEO? What was that man like? So, far she'd seen no difference, but would that continue once the real world invaded?

Why was she even thinking about this? He'd invited her because he needed a date and she was convenient. He seemed to really care about her, but she knew it wouldn't be long until he realized he was done with her. She'd enjoy the dream while it lasted, and as soon as they got to the party, she'd disappear into the wall and he'd never even notice.

GABE PRESSED his hand into the small of Livy's back as they entered the restaurant. It was his favorite, and the chef was one of his closest friends. The maître d' seated them at a cozy booth near the back of the restaurant, and Gabe slid into the booth beside her.

One of the reasons he'd wanted to eat out was because he could tell she was a little uncomfortable with his lifestyle, and he wanted to show her that he was still just Gabe and she *did* fit in his world. The restaurant he'd picked was an incredible one, but she'd meet one of his friends and see that the number of zeros in his bank account didn't affect who he was as a person.

"Long time no see, Gabe Saxon." His friend Tyler Clayton extended a hand, and he shook it. "And who, may I ask, is the beautiful woman with the fetching gray eyes?"

Livy's cheeks turned a soft shade of pink, and she smiled.

"Tyler Clayton, this is Olivia Weber. Olivia, this is my friend, well, my closest friend, Tyler. He's the chef."

Tyler sat on the bench across from them and shook her hand. "It's nice to meet you, Olivia Weber."

"Nice to meet you."

His friend kept his gaze on Livy. "Are you the reason my buddy isn't working himself to death?"

"I don't know."

"She is," Gabe said and put his arm around her, pulling her close.

Tyler laughed. "Well, then I need to thank you." He sobered. "You're looking better. I was worried the last time I saw you."

"Yeah."

Livy leaned forward. "Worried?"

"My friend here was working himself into the ground. The last time I saw him, death would've looked better."

Gabe rolled his eyes. It was true, but Tyler didn't need to tell Livy that. "Cut that out."

Tyler turned his attention back to Livy and narrowed his eyes. "You love baked seafood. Scallops being your favorite."

Her mouth dropped open. "It's my favorite. How did you do that?"

"It's a gift. Is that what you want tonight?"

She nodded. "I'd love it."

"How about you, Gabe? The usual?"

"Yeah." He paused. "Ty, there's a dinner party this weekend at the Lake George house. You game?"

Tyler nodded and stood. "I'm game. See you there." Tyler smiled at Livy. "It was lovely meeting you." Tipping his head, he said, "Gabe." Then he walked away.

"He was nice," Livy said.

Gabe smiled. "He's a great guy. One of the few in my circle that keeps his feet on the ground."

"Did you all grow up here in the city?"

"Yeah, I've known him my whole life. I don't have many close friends. I closed down last year, and most of the people I called friends at the time didn't stick around. He did."

"I like him. Not sure how he knew seafood was my favorite, but that was a neat trick."

"His food is fantastic. He wasn't kidding when he said he was gifted." Gabe leaned down and put his lips to her ear. "And he said you were beautiful too, so now you can't say it was just me being nice."

She giggled and looked down. "I did say he was nice."

Pulling back, he used one finger to lift her chin up. As he held her gaze, he said, "And just as honest as I am."

He brought her lips to his and immediately deepened the kiss, wrapping his arms around her and filling the remaining space between them. Her fingers tangled in his hair, making it seem as though she was as desperate for him as he was for her.

"Gabe, *what* are you doing?" Rachelle's voice pierced through the moment, and they broke apart. He looked up and found her standing with her arms crossed over her chest. "And *why* is your mouth on another woman?"

"I told you it was over, so the whereabouts of my mouth is none of your business."

Her eyes narrowed. "You were serious?"

"Yeah, I was serious. We are done. There is no us. There never will be an us ever again." He looked at Livy and smiled. Her eyes were wide, but he didn't get the feeling that she was upset. More like confused as to why Rachelle had shown up out of the blue. "Now, if you don't mind, I'm having dinner with a beautiful woman, and I'd appreciate it if you left me alone."

"If you're doing this to make me jealous, it's working."

Gabe laughed and looked back up at her. "I don't care what you are, Rachelle, as long as whatever it is remains far away from me. Goodbye."

"Gabe." The way she said his name would have had him taking her into his arms just a month ago. "We've been together most of our lives. You'd throw that away? For...her?"

"That was the problem. I was with you, but you were never with me. I'm done. Just leave me alone. You threw it away when you left me at the altar for the other man."

Her arms dropped. "But this is how we are."

"Not anymore."

Rachelle turned her cold eyes on Livy. "Let me guess. He's given you the story of how wounded he is and how badly I've treated him. How he lost his poor dad and nearly worked himself to death. Well, let me just tell you that there's a lot more to Gabriel Saxon that he's telling you. Watch yourself. Woman to woman, he'll break your heart and make you bleed." She turned on her heels and stormed off.

Gabe turned to Livy. He could only imagine what she was thinking. "I'm sorry."

He thought he saw a flash of doubt cross her face as he looked at her, but it was so quick that he hoped he imagined it. She wouldn't believe anything Rachelle had said, would she?

"It's okay." Livy smiled. "At least she didn't climb onto a tabletop and declare her undying love while trying to recreate the scene from Top Gun by singing

'You've Lost that Lovin' Feeling.' Trust me, when Jacob did that, it was far worse than this."

He threw his head back and laughed. "He didn't."

"Oh, he did. Badly. I swear there are cats in heat that can sing better."

Still laughing, he said, "Okay, that's bad. Rachelle doesn't care a whit about me. I'm surprised she even went to the trouble of coming over here."

"How did she even know you were here?"

He shrugged. "Our social circle frequents this restaurant regularly. It's the best. I'm guessing one of her friends saw me with you and called her."

She shivered. "That's a little creepy."

"A little, and had I thought a little deeper I would have been prepared for it."

"What is it with crazy exes?"

Gabe chuckled. "I have no idea."

Livy laid her head against his chest and hugged him around the waist. "I'm glad she was crazy."

On that, they could agree. Jacob had been so stupid, and Gabe would never be able to thank him enough.

He pulled her legs over his lap and wrapped his arms around her. There had to be a future in which she was a permanent fixture in his life. He couldn't picture living without her anymore.

Once the dinner party was over and things had settled down again, he was going to talk to her about where she saw them going. What he saw was marriage, children, and a million anniversaries. He hoped she shared his vision.

CHAPTER 18

*L*ivy had spent the night before and most of the morning replaying the entire evening at the restaurant. Rachelle was Livy's polar opposite —well dressed, poised, and completely at home in Gabe's world. How could Gabe look at Livy and not wish he was with someone better?

But, the way he'd kissed her. It was magical and wonderful and everything she'd ever wanted in a kiss. Soul-searing. Whatever happened, there would never be another man who would affect her like Gabe.

Then Rachelle had given that little speech which had caused a seriously sleepless night. At no point had what she said lined up with the man Livy had been spending time with. Of course, Jacob had deceived her for a long time, and she'd been slow to catch on. But when she looked into Gabe's eyes, her heart said he was telling the truth. Then again, how many times had her heart led her astray?

Now, she was in a ritzy store, trying on a dress that made her feel completely out of place. And she wasn't even at the party yet. "Gabe, I don't know that I'm cut out—" Livy looked up as she exited the dressing room, and her eyes widened.

A slender woman with silver hair stood next to Gabe. She was tall, impeccably dressed in a dark green wrap-around dress with black heels, and every bit the sophisticated woman Livy had expected to see while she was in the city. There was no denying she was Gabe's mom. The woman smiled and extended a hand to Livy. "I'm Mildred Saxon, but you can call me Millie."

"Hi, I'm Olivia Weber. You can call me Livy."

"It's nice to meet you. You're simply stunning."

The dress Livy had tried on stopped just above her knees, hugged her curves, and swooped low in the back. It covered all the right parts, but she wasn't comfortable in it at all.

"Gabe did say you were lovely, and he wasn't kidding. I'm so glad to meet you."

Livy tucked a piece of hair behind her ear. "He's very sweet."

His mom turned her attention to Gabe who was gaping. "Yes, he is." His mom lifted an eyebrow. "Gabe, love, put your tongue back in your mouth."

Livy giggled and rolled her lips in, but there was no hiding her smile.

His neck turned red as he closed his mouth, and it traveled up to his face.

"I don't wear dresses very often, and I feel weird in this one."

His mom turned her around and walked with her to the floor-length mirror. "I think it looks great, but if you aren't comfortable in it, don't wear it. You can't spend hours in a dress when it's driving you insane."

"I'm not uncomfortable exactly, just…"

"Exposed?"

Livy nodded. "There's not a lot of fabric here."

His mom squeezed her shoulders. "Hold on. Let me see if I can find something."

"Okay."

Gabe approached her while his mom hunted through the racks of dresses. "You may not be comfortable in it, but you sure look fantastic."

She waved him off and shook her head.

He tipped her chin up, and his eyes locked with hers. "Don't do that." His voice was husky, and the intensity of his stare made her knees weak.

His mom cleared her throat. "Why don't you try this one on?"

"Okay." Heat rushed to her cheeks as Gabe dropped his hand, and she took the dress and hurried back to the dressing room, shutting the door behind her.

What she wouldn't give to be a fly on the wall out there with Gabe and his mom. What did she think of Livy? What if his mom thought she wasn't good enough? Would he send her home? What if his mother thought that and he just didn't tell her? She shook her head, trying to clear the thoughts. No. Gabe was honest, and she trusted him.

She pulled the short, tight dress off and stepped into the one his mom had picked with hopes that it would work. Once she got it on, she stared at herself in the mirror. The floor-length silver gown had a square neckline with capped sleeves. The bodice was body-hugging down to her hips where the organza skirt flared out. Livy turned to see the back, and it swooped like the other, but it didn't make her feel nearly as naked.

Livy paused at the dressing room door and then stepped out. She stopped just past the door and waited for them to finish talking. They'd turned their backs, caught up in a lively discussion.

When Gabe turned, his eyes widened. "Wow."

His mom stepped forward and pulled Livy's hair up as she turned her toward the mirror. "Oh, honey, is this the one?"

"I really like it. It's comfortable, and I don't feel weird in it. Thank you. I don't think I would have picked it since it was long. Usually, they're *too* long for me." It had been a long time since someone felt motherly toward her.

Millie let her hair drop and squeezed her shoulders. "Well, this one seems to be just right. Do you wear heels or flats?"

"Flats."

Millie smiled. "Would kitten heels be okay?"

"I hadn't thought of that. Those would be okay."

"You wear, what? A size six?"

Livy chuckled. "And a half."

"Would it be okay if I tried to find you some?"

His mom was so kind. She could soak up this kind of attention and never be full. "I'd love that."

Gabe waited for his mom to leave and then approached her. "You look beautiful."

"Thank you. Does that mean you like it?"

"I think you look fantastic in anything you wear, but I have to say, in that dress, you are downright stunning."

Her cheeks grew so hot she was sure they were going to set the building on fire. "You're so sweet."

He ran his fingertips down her bare spine, letting his hand come to rest on the small of her back. Pulling her to him, he said, "Thank you for agreeing to be my date."

Livy didn't know what to say. She'd never met anyone like Gabe before. She'd spent the past week reevaluating her value. He thought she was worth something. Not that she needed a man to give that to her, but he'd shown her how she should be treated, and having that comparison was slowly changing her own perceptions of herself and what she should expect from someone who cared about her.

"Livy?"

Livy peered around Gabe as Tori bounded into the boutique. "Hey, Tori."

"Don't you look like the bell of the ball. That's some dress, girlfriend." She looked from Livy to Gabe. "And," she said sticking her hand out, "it's good to finally meet you in person. I'm Tori Bennett."

Gabe shook her hand. "It's nice to meet you. Gabriel Saxon. Call me Gabe."

Tori let her gaze sweep from Gabe back to Livy. "I can't believe you're going to a party. My little wallflower is branching out."

"Stop it."

Millie walked up holding two different pairs of shoes. "Oh, hello."

"This is my agent, Tori Bennett. Tori, this is Gabe's mom, Millie Saxon."

Tori smiled. "Hi, it's nice to meet you."

His mom smiled at Tori. "Likewise." She turned to Livy. "Want to try these on?"

Livy took them from her and set both pairs on the floor. She tried on one and then the other. The first one was the better, so she chose those. "Well, I guess I'm done."

"You look great, Liv," Tori said.

"Gabe's mom picked it out. I really like it." She ran her hand down the front of the dress. It was so pretty, and it gave her a confidence boost. She felt special in it. "I'm going to go change. I'll be right back."

Before she could move, Gabe pulled her close and kissed her. "You really do look beautiful."

Tori snorted. "Oh, we so need to talk."

Millie bumped Tori's shoulder. "I told Gabe the same thing."

Gabe didn't even flinch. He just kept his eyes on Livy. "Go get changed, and we'll get some lunch."

Livy nodded and walked to the dressing room. Shutting the door behind her, she covered her face with her hands. Oh, she was in so much trouble. Gabe had money, social status, and so many other things that made her wonder how it could ever possibly work. He was so out of her league, and she was falling for him. Was falling? Had fallen. If Gabe threw her away, she'd be shattered. She felt secure with him. More than she'd ever felt with anyone. She was safe in his arms, and more than anything she hoped her heart was safe with him too.

THE RESTAURANT MILLIE picked for lunch was bright and open. It felt very feminine and dainty. Gabe's mom had convinced him to go get a tuxedo that would complement her dress, so it was just Millie and Livy. Tori had been invited, but she'd claimed she had a business lunch to attend. More than likely, she'd realized what Millie wanted, which was to talk to Livy alone.

Gabe was her son, and it would only be natural to want to protect him after the way Rachelle had treated him.

"So, I hope you won't be mad at Gabe, but he told me your pen name."

Livy wiped her mouth and set down her fork. The

salad she'd ordered was filling, and if she took another bite, she'd pop. "Oh, there are exceptions to secrets. Moms are one of them."

Millie chuckled. "That's good to know."

"Thank you for finding that dress and those shoes. They're perfect. I would've never found them without you."

"Oh, honey, it's fun. Kath and I go shopping once a week just to try on stuff. Just to give us a chance to spend time together and catch up."

Livy tried hard to remember her mom, but everything was so fuzzy now. "I bet that's fun."

"How about you? Any family?"

She shook her head. "No. Well, I have twin sisters, but I don't know much about them. My parents died when I was young, and I grew up in the foster system."

His mom's lips parted with a soft gasp. "Oh, honey, I'm so sorry."

"It's okay."

"You don't know anything about your sisters?"

"No. I tried to find them, but they weren't really interested in meeting me, so I didn't push it." She'd never been so free with that information before, but it was as though Gabe had been a key and the locked door now stood wide open.

Millie's eyebrows knitted together, and she

stretched her hand across the table, covering Livy's. "From what I can tell, they're missing out."

"That's very sweet."

She pulled her hand back and smiled. "Gabe really likes you."

Livy looked down. "He's so kind. I've never met anyone like him before."

"He's the sweetest man you'll ever meet. He's so much like his father. Daniel had the kindest, sweetest heart. He'd give the shirt off his back to take care of someone. Albert renting you that cabin? Most people would have fired him, but not my Gabe."

"He never did tell me about that."

His mom took the silver heart pendant that hung around her neck between her fingers. "Albert's niece needed a kidney transplant. He is a very proud man and didn't ask for help. He should have. The man is more like family. Gabe is taking care of all her medical care and providing for her medication once she leaves the hospital."

A new level of affection for Gabe bloomed in Livy. She knew he was kind, but that was beyond generous. "I'm not surprised he'd do that."

"He does that kind of thing more than most. Rachelle almost killed that part of him. She wasn't good for him."

Livy nodded. "She was hateful to him. I don't understand why. Then she showed up while we were having dinner last night and seemed shocked that he'd be with someone else."

"Oh, that's Rachelle. The woman thinks the world should revolve around her. I was so glad when she left him. It broke my heart to see him hurt, but I knew she'd make him miserable. He overlooked so much and made excuses for her. She didn't deserve my Gabe."

She smiled. "No, I don't think so either. He said he collapsed a couple of months ago."

"He did. I knew he wasn't doing well, but he was so driven. I don't know what was behind it, but there was this feverish, almost desperate desire to prove himself. He didn't need to. Anyone who loved him knew he was wonderful."

"What happened?"

"He was working to buy this little publishing house. They'd had some success with a few indie writers, and they were insistent on dealing with Gabe. Of course, that wasn't the only deal he was working on. At the time, it was one of more than a handful. He was working nonstop." His mom took her pendant in her fingers again and rubbed it. "During a meeting, he just fell to the floor. He was so pale, and his heart was beating erratically."

Livy moved seats until she was sitting next to Millie. "I'm so sorry."

"He probably thinks I didn't know, but I knew he was close to collapsing again. I made him take some time away because he'd pushed himself too hard. We lost his father to a heart attack, and I'm so afraid of losing him too."

Livy put her arm around his mom's shoulders. "I can't imagine how that must hurt you." It hurt hearing it the first time from Gabe, but hearing his mom speak about it broke her heart.

"He doesn't need to prove anything. He's a good man."

"I think so too."

Millie patted her hand. "Thank you." Then she brightened when she looked past Livy.

Livy looked over her shoulder as a woman approached the table. "This is my daughter, Kath."

Kath extended a hand to Livy, and she shook it. "Hi, I'm sorry I'm late. We had a little bit of a crisis at the shelter." The family resemblance was striking. Kath was a younger version of Millie, only with Gabe's dark hair. Her features were just as delicate as her mom's.

"Shelter?" Livy asked as Kath sat down.

Gabe's sister nodded. "I run a private homeless shelter."

This family was amazing. Were they all this generous? "That's…kind of amazing. What brought that about?"

"I was a little lost for a while after my dad died. It gives me purpose and a way to show how grateful I am for what I have." Kath smiled. The waitress stopped at the table, and she ordered a sandwich and a bottle of water. "I can't stay long. I've got to get back."

Livy nodded. "Sure. Could I come see it?"

Kath's eyes sparkled as her gaze drifted from Livy to her mom. "I'm always up for showing people around. I'll warn you, though, there's a chance you'll get put to work."

"Really? Okay."

"You want to come, Mom?"

Millie nodded. "Can we stop at the house so I can change?"

"You bet."

This was a family Livy could find herself immersed in. It was the family she'd longed for since her parents died.

Little doubts tickled in the back of her mind. What if the little bubble they'd had at the cabin was about to burst and he was only keeping her around until the party was over and the deal was announced? This taste of so much good was heaven, but nothing good ever lasted for Livy.

She could enjoy herself at the moment, but she needed to remember to keep her feet on the ground. If she didn't, there was a good chance she'd be crushed.

CHAPTER 19

"Thank you for inviting me to dinner," Tori said. "Even though you were doing it for Livy." She gave Livy a smile and a wink.

Gabe cast his gaze to the table. It was true. Livy had mentioned in passing that she wanted Tori to try Tyler's restaurant, and he enjoyed seeing her happy. He'd done it for other reasons too. One of them being that he liked Tori. She spoke her mind, and he liked that.

"Actually, that's not the only reason," he said.

Tori narrowed her eyes as she looked at him. "Oh?"

"I've done a little research on you, and your track record is fantastic. You can pick a story, and your authors are doing well." He slid his arm around Livy's waist and pulled her close as a punctuation mark. "I'm offering you an acquisitions position in Saxon. I know I can match what you're currently making, if not beat it."

She looked from him to Livy. "Did you have something to do with this?"

Livy shook her head. "No, I had no idea. I'm finding out right now."

"I'll have to think about it. I actually love what I do." She smiled. "There's a rush in seeing a query pop up in my email. Of getting those first few pages and seeing the potential. I'm not sure I could leave that."

"I can see your point."

"It wouldn't be the same being in acquisitions. I'd be getting what another agent thought was good, and sometimes they pass on things they shouldn't. They let what they want override what the readers want. I'm good at what I do because I follow what people are reading."

"That's smart."

"I hate to interrupt, but I need to use the restroom," Livy said.

Gabe stood and let her out of the booth.

Livy looked at Tori. "No stories while I'm gone."

Tori snickered. "We're talking business. Go away."

With a playful huff, she walked away.

The moment she disappeared from view, Tori said, "You're in love with her."

Gabe's heart raced as he brought his gaze to hers and held it. What could he say? He hadn't even used that word in his thoughts yet. He wouldn't confirm it when his mother said it. That word was hard for him. Once he spoke it, there would be no denying what he felt for her. Was there any denying it anyway? Just because he was afraid of using the word didn't mean he didn't feel it.

Was he afraid of the word, or was he afraid of saying it and Livy not returning his love? Deep down, he'd always known Rachelle didn't love him. If Livy didn't love him, he'd be devastated. He'd never wanted someone's love as much as he wanted hers.

"I can't blame you. I've always told her that when the right guy came along, he'd never let her go."

He nodded and wondered if Livy thought he was the right guy. If she'd have him, he'd never leave her. Spending time with her had changed him. It had reminded him of what he wanted. A family. Someone to hold and love. Children to swing and play ball with. And all of what he wanted started with Livy.

"Thank you for buying that dress too. There's no way she could have afforded it."

His eyebrows knitted together. "What? She makes six figures easily."

"She does, but she lives on fifty thousand a year."

"What? Why?"

"Don't tell her I told you this, but she gives all of what she makes minus the little bit she keeps to live on to a children's home in Orlando."

Gabe wasn't floored. He was moved. His dad would have loved her. "I don't think I'm surprised."

"She's told you what happened to her as a kid. That's not a question. It's a fact."

He didn't know if he should confirm or deny what Tori said, so he just kept quiet.

"I can see it in the way she looks at you. That was a big deal for her, and you should know that you're the only one she's ever shared that with."

He nodded and then looked her in the eyes. "She's safe with me."

"I've done research on you too. She's been due something good for a long time. I just hope you realize what you've got. Please don't hurt her."

"I don't plan on it."

Tori pulled her gaze from his and smiled. "Hey, Liv."

"Hey. Please tell me you didn't tell any stories."

"Of course. What good would it be to be left alone with him if I didn't?"

Her eyes widened as Gabe stood to let her back into the seat. "Oh gosh. Should I be embarrassed?"

Gabe shook his head. "Nope."

"Are you just being nice?"

"I'm back in New York. I'm ruthless here."

Her gaze caught his, and her big gray eyes seemed to look through him. "Well, we know that isn't possible."

Tori cleared her throat. "Still here."

Livy's cheeks turned an adorable shade of pink that matched her lips. It made him wish Tori wasn't there because a peck on the lips wouldn't be satisfactory.

He held Livy's gaze a moment longer. Love wasn't nearly as dangerous when he was with her. If she wanted his heart, she could have it. If he was honest, she already had it.

He was in love with her, and his desire to find out where she stood burned brighter. After the dinner party, he was going to find out. He knew her tendency to overanalyze, and he didn't want there to be any excuses. When he told her he loved her, he wanted her to be able to hear him. Whatever it took, however loud he needed to speak, he'd do it.

STRETCHING, Livy turned in Gabe's arms as they lay in front of the fire. Even with the fingerprint security, he'd made a thick pallet of blankets in the living room, seeming to pick up on her nervousness about being alone in the guest room. Not fearful, but anxious. Plus, she loved their nightly fireplace cuddling.

Her day had been so full that it was nice to have a moment to relax. Spending the day with Kath and Millie at the homeless shelter had been exhilarating. The more she learned about Gabe's family, the more she wanted to tie herself to it. This was the family she was desperate for. The kind she wanted loving her.

Then Gabe had surprised her by meeting Tori at his friend Tyler's restaurant. He had no idea what that meant to her. It had been a passing comment that she wanted Tori to try it, and he'd heard her. He was such a special man.

"Your sister is incredible," Livy said. "And your arranging dinner with Tori...I can't believe you did that."

Gabe kissed her neck and nuzzled it with his nose. "You've said that already."

"I know, but no one has been as wonderful to me as

you have." She paused a moment and touched her lips to his. "And you should have seen your sister. She was so gentle and kind. The way she treats everyone with such dignity and grace. And then there's you."

He pulled back. "Me?"

"Your taking care of Albert's niece. You are a wonderful man, Gabe Saxon."

"Not that special."

"Yes, you are. There aren't a lot of people who would have done what you did. It would have been so easy to condemn Albert, and you didn't."

He shrugged. "He's family, and he needed help."

"Yes, but that homeless shelter isn't family, and you support it too."

"Kath gets donations from several people."

"You purchased the building, you pay the taxes, and you bought all her supplies to get it started."

Gabe grumbled. "She shouldn't have told you that."

"She was bragging about you. She's incredibly proud of you. Both your mom and your sister are, and with good reason." She took his face in her hands, holding his gaze. "You are a sweet man. There is no doubt in my mind that your dad was extremely proud of you. He may have disagreed with the direction you chose, but that was a disagreement. He was absolutely proud of the man you are. There's no way he couldn't have been."

His dark eyes took on the intense stare that typically unnerved her. "You think so? You think Rachelle was lying to me?"

"She had to have been. She was just being cruel because she knew it would hurt you."

He nodded. "Thank you. I wanted him to be proud of me. My dad was a good man, and I wanted to emulate him."

"I'd say mission accomplished."

The smile he shot her was sweet and full of warmth. Not the knee-weakening or hair-melting kind, but the kind that said thank you. "From anyone else, it would mean nothing, and I wouldn't believe them. Coming from you, it means everything."

His family wasn't what she expected at all. Like herself, they took their money and gave it back to the people who needed it instead of hoarding it for large yachts. Sure, having nice things was okay, but there needed to be a balance. Millie and Kath were both amazing, and she couldn't wait to meet his brothers and their families. If they were anything like his mom and sister, she expected them to be wonderful.

She curled her hands under her chin as he pulled her close and kissed the top of her head. Snuggling into him was amazing. Gabe was a good, decent man, and anyone who thought any different was crazy.

He was her knight in shining armor. The one she didn't know she'd been waiting for. He was showing her that she should expect more from the people in her life. Scraps weren't enough anymore.

CHAPTER 20

A scream pulled Gabe from a deep sleep. Then another blood-curdling scream had him flying off the bed toward Livy's room. They'd driven to his family's Lake George home that day to have a moment alone before his family descended on the place. He'd spent the last two days sharing Livy, and while he loved that his mom and sister had welcomed Livy so openly, he'd missed it just being the two of them.

When he reached her bedroom, the door was open, and the room was empty. She screamed again, and he realized it was coming from the family room. He raced down the hall and down the stairs, through the formal living room to the back of the house, and stopped as he reached the doorway.

Livy was wedged into a corner with her hands in front of her face. Moonlight was streaming through the windows, and he could see that her cheeks were wet.

He crossed the room and knelt in front of her. "Livy," he said, taking her hands. "Livy. You're safe."

She swatted at him and covered her head with her arms. "I won't go with you. I won't."

"Olivia." This time he took her by the waist and pulled her to him. "You're safe. I won't let anyone hurt you."

Her little body trembled as he embraced her, and she wrapped her arms around his neck so tight he struggled to breathe, burying her face in his shoulder.

"It's okay. I've got you."

Gabe stood, swept his arms under her legs, and took her to the couch, sinking into it with her sitting in his lap. Sobs shook her, and she sucked in air, fighting to breathe. By the time she'd calmed enough to relax against him, he had no idea how long she'd clung to him as he whispered reassurances to her.

"I'm so sorry," she said and hiccupped.

He rubbed his hands up and down her back. "You have nothing to be sorry for. You had a nightmare. It's okay."

She pulled back and used the hem of her shirt to wipe her face. "It's been a while since I had one."

He cupped her cheek. "What caused you to have the nightmare?"

"I've just been thinking a lot about things. Michael, all the foster homes I went through. Your mom and sister have been so good to me. I guess I just feel… robbed now that I've spent time with them." She sniffed.

"I can see how that might affect you."

She touched her forehead to his. "I came in here because I couldn't sleep and I didn't want to wake you up. I feel awful."

"Why?"

"Because I know you need rest too. I don't want you to be sick again." She leaned back.

He was tongue-tied. There had never been a moment when Rachelle ever cared about what her actions did to him. "I'm feeling better than I have in a long time. Sleeping until I wake up. Spending time with you. I'm okay."

"Are you sure? Your mom was so worried about you. She really loves you. When you collapsed, you scared her. Losing your dad made her afraid of losing you too."

His mom was afraid of losing him? He'd never even considered that. "She is?"

Livy nodded.

He rested his hand on her back. "I didn't even think of that. I had a heart arrhythmia. It's fine now, but I had to take medication to fix it."

For a heartbeat, she stared at him as if he'd tried to jump off a bridge. "You have to take care of yourself. You can't work that hard anymore. I know you think you need to prove yourself, but you don't. Your family adores you. They're so proud of you. You should hear the way your sister and mom talk about you."

A smile spread on his lips. "They are?"

"Well yeah. You're not just great at your job, you're a great person, Gabe. Of course they're proud of you."

He'd been killing himself because he thought he needed validation. "Thank you for telling me that."

"I should have told you earlier. It didn't occur to me that you didn't know."

Gabe smiled. The talk he'd been wanting to have with her was on the tip of his tongue, but he wanted his brothers to meet her first. They weren't coming in until the next day, and then the next couple of days they'd be preparing for the party. When he talked to her, he didn't want anything else on his mind but the two of them. "When this party is over, I think we need to talk."

She hugged him and laid her head on his chest. "Okay."

DINNER WAS a serious affair in the Saxon family. The dining room—not the formal one as that one was three times the size of this one and was meant for parties like the one coming up—held a table large enough to seat twelve people, and every seat was filled since Gabe's nieces and nephews were included. His brothers each had two children, and Peter's wife was expecting their third at the beginning of spring.

The way the family interacted was something out of one of her novels. They teased one another, shared what was going on in their lives, and seemed genuinely thrilled to see one another. If she could paint a picture of a perfect family, it would be them. Her temptation would be to draw herself into it.

Gabe wanted to talk after the party. She'd snuggled close to him so he didn't see her face. Anytime someone wanted to talk to her, it usually meant they wanted to say goodbye. She didn't want to say goodbye, but she'd learned a long time ago that when someone was done with her, they were done.

Livy glanced around as she sat between Gabe and Kath.

Kath leaned over and whispered, "Can you say chaos?"

With a laugh, Livy said, "I think it's great."

"Just wait until you've been subjected to dozens of these. It won't seem so great then."

If Kath only knew what Livy would give to be at all of them. "I don't know. It's pretty funny."

Peter, sitting next to Gabe, leaned forward and looked at Livy. "Has Gabe told you about the summer he decided he was a skateboarder?"

Gabe's face turned beet red. "She doesn't need to hear that."

"I disagree. I think I need to hear that," Livy said as she winked at Gabe.

His brother's lips twitched up, and he smiled so wide his teeth peeked through. "Okay, let me set the scene. Gabe has just turned seven, and Mom and Dad have taken us to this dude ranch in Arizona."

Brendan snorted. "Oh man. I forgot about that."

Gabe hung his head. "Ugh, please don't."

"So, anyway," Peter continues. "The house on this dude ranch has this long porch, and at the end of it, there are these cactuses. Not a whole lot, but enough that you know to steer clear."

Gabe groaned, and his head dropped onto the back of his chair. "No."

"About three days before we leave, Gabe decides he's going to skateboard off this porch and over those cactuses."

Livy snorted and pressed her fingers to her lips. She could see in her mind what was coming, and it was all she could do not to cackle. "Oh no."

"Oh yeah. He pushes off, and he's tearing down this porch. When he gets to the end, he kicks up, but he doesn't have enough momentum and plummets into the middle of them. Butt first."

Livy clasped both her hands over her mouth, trying to hold in the laugh and failed. "Oh no."

"He looked like a dog who'd lost a fight with a porcupine."

Millie snickered. "It took me hours to pull all of those needles out."

"He couldn't sit for a week," Kath said, wiping tears as they ran down her cheeks.

Gabe exhaled and wouldn't meet her eyes. "To this day, I hate cactuses."

Livy touched his arm. "Oh, I bet that was awful."

"It was my own stupid fault. Dad tried to tell me

the porch wasn't long enough, but I just wouldn't listen. Lesson learned, but, man, was it a hard lesson." Gabe chuckled.

"I can't imagine," Livy said.

"You listened to your dad a lot better after that," Millie said and pointed her finger at him.

Gabe snorted. "Yes, I did."

Brendan cleared his throat. "So, Livy, where are you from?"

"Orlando."

"Do you like living there?" he asked.

How could she answer that? It was familiar, but it wasn't home. Not really. "Uh, it's okay. I like the beach. I could do without the traffic. The summers are the worst with all the tourists."

Brendan nodded. "I hadn't thought of that, but I bet that would be a nightmare."

"What do you do for a living?" Peter asked.

This was Gabe's family. She was going to be honest with them. If her pen name got out, she'd just deal with it. "I'm an author. Well, a romance author. I write under the name Amelia Hurst."

Brendan's wife, Lauren, dropped her fork and leaned forward as Peter's wife, Krista, looked at Livy with her eyes wide. "You're Amelia Hurst?" Lauren asked.

Livy nodded. "Yeah."

"You know her?" Brendan asked.

Lauren's eyes widened, and she looked at her husband as if he'd grown a third head. "Uh, yeah. She's only the best romance author there is." She returned her gaze to Livy. "I have one of your books with me. Do you think you could sign it?"

"Sure."

Krista grinned. "I have a couple of them with me. Would you sign mine too?"

"Of course."

"That's awesome. Thank you," Krista said.

Livy tucked a piece of hair behind her ear, and her cheeks heated. Being the center of attention took her out of her comfort zone, but she was happy to sign their books.

Gabe leaned down and put his lips to her ear. "You didn't have to tell them who you are."

"I know. I wanted to."

"I know that was hard for you." He touched his cheek to hers. "Thank you."

"You're welcome."

Being with his family...the way they'd accepted her with open arms filled her with joy. What would Thanksgiving with them be like? It sure would beat her frozen dinner. And Christmas? She could see it so clearly. A huge decorated tree with presents stacked underneath, this family all gathered together talking and laughing…if she got nothing but the chance to be with them, it would be the best Christmas ever.

But he wanted to talk. Her heart broke as the vision of a family-filled Christmas faded, and past Christmases of her alone, sitting in front of the TV watching *A Christmas Story*, floated to mind. At least she'd have this memory for a while, and she'd cherish it. Having just a taste was hard because she wanted it all the time, but she'd take what she got.

This experience had taught her that she wanted more out of life, and Gabe had taught her that she was worthy to be loved. She wasn't sure she'd ever be able to love someone as much as she loved Gabe, but she knew that she was done settling for less.

CHAPTER 21

*L*ivy wasn't accustomed to getting her hair, fingernails, and toenails done. Well, she wasn't accustomed to going to parties either, so none of it was all that familiar to her. Still, the pampering was fun. More than anything, spending time with the Saxon women was a blast. They were all really close and seemed to genuinely enjoy each other's company.

"Millie, thanks for getting Rebecca to come babysit on such short notice. When Elena called and told me she was sick, I thought for sure I'd be missing the dinner party," Krista said.

Gabe's mom waved her off. "Oh, honey, it was nothing. I love Henry and Samantha, but a woman needs to have a break from time to time and spend the evening dressed up with her husband. I could tell you needed a break."

"Oh, you have no idea. Henry has decided he likes sharpies. I have been running around behind him like a chicken with its head cut off. He tried to highlight Sam's hair with one. I caught him just before he put the pen to it."

Lauren rolled her head to look at Krista. "Oh, Jack is in his 'I don't want to' phase. I swear, sometimes I think he's the reason wine was invented."

"Do you have any children, Livy?" asked Kath.

Her eyes widened. "Oh, no. I want some one day, but I'm not in a rush."

"Me too. Although, sometimes after family affairs such as this, I question my desire." Kath held up her hand. "Don't get me wrong. I love Henry, Sam, Caroline, and Jack, but some of these stories make my hair stand on end."

Krista snorted. "Oh, they can be terrors, but then when they crawl into your lap and hug you or hold your face and tell you they love you, it's the best feeling in the world," she said and palmed her stomach.

Livy smiled. "Do you know what you're having yet?"

"Another boy. Ethan Smith. Ethan is my grandfather's name."

"I like that name," Livy said.

"Yeah, my grandfather is a tough old coot. He's determined to see this one born."

Livy's eyebrows slowly rose. "How old is he?"

"My due date is on his one-hundredth birthday."

"I bet he's tickled."

Krista chuckled. "The moment I told him, he said, 'Well, then I guess his name is Ethan.' I couldn't say no. I'm just glad Peter loves me enough to go with it."

"Ethan's a great name."

"Yes, but Peter had it in his head that he was going to name him Lando."

Livy tilted her head. "That's an unusual name."

"It's from *Star Wars*. Lando Calrissian."

All of them burst out laughing with Kath nearly in tears. "That's Peter. You'd think he'd grow out of his *Star Wars* phase," Millie said once they calmed down.

Krista shook her head. "You'd think, but no. That's why we have a house with a basement, so he can do his *Star Wars* thing down there."

Lauren chuckled. "Oh, don't think you're alone. Brendan is now a microbrewer."

Millie snorted. "A what?"

"A microbrewer, as in beer. And let me tell you, failure stinks. Our garage needs a scent exorcism."

Gabe's mom pressed her fingers to her chest and shook with laughter. "Oh, that boy of mine."

The stories continued for the rest of the afternoon. Livy hadn't laughed so hard in a long time, other than her snowball fight with Gabe, but this was different. They made her feel welcomed and part of their circle. They didn't know Gabe didn't want to keep her around, and she didn't want to spoil anything.

She would never forget her time with this family or these incredibly witty and interesting women. They had a confidence in who they were that Livy had never achieved, but as she sat listening to them, she realized their confidence didn't come from outside sources or dependence on the opinions of others. They were confident because they knew who they were.

It made Livy take stock of who she was. Was she the mistreated orphan that she'd always seen herself as, or was she something else? Why had she hung on to that identity so long? Maybe it was time to stop being that scared little girl. Why had she given so many people who didn't love her so much power over who she was? It was past time to shuck off that part of her life and realize that there was more to life than living in the past.

A KNOCK on the bedroom door drew Gabe away from the mirror and the accursed tie he couldn't seem to get straight. He opened the door, and his sister stepped in. "Having trouble?"

"This stupid tie. I hate them."

Kath slapped his hand and began fixing it. "I love Livy. She's the complete opposite of Rachelle."

He looked up as her fingers pulled on his collar. "Yes, she is."

"Mom says you're in love with her. Are you?"

"Yeah. Madly and deeply."

Kath pulled on his tie one last time. "There. Done."

Gabe walked to the mirror to check it. "Thanks."

"Have you told her?"

"No, I wanted to talk to her after the party was over. I wanted this announcement done and nothing else on my mind when I did."

"Are you sure you weren't wanting confirmation from us that you weren't getting yourself into another Rachelle situation?"

"Maybe, but I did want Peter and Brendan to meet

her first. If she's going to be a part of this family, you guys needed to meet her."

"Well, we all think she's great."

Gabe chuckled and turned from the mirror to look at his sister. "Did you take a poll?"

"No, but we did talk. You haven't been this happy in a long time. She's good for you." Kath walked to him and hugged him.

He returned the hug. "Thanks, Kath."

"I'll see you at the party. I hear Tyler's coming."

Gabe winked.

She giggled and left his room.

Kath was the other reason he'd invited Tyler. They'd had a flame for each other for a while, and he hoped the party would fan the flames a little.

As he slipped on his coat, he checked himself in the mirror one last time before leaving his room. Livy was two doors down, and he hadn't seen her since breakfast. He stopped at her door and rapped his knuckles against it.

The door opened, and time stopped. Her beauty was beyond words. Her hair was pulled up, and little tendrils framed her face. The only makeup he could see was the little bit that brought out her eyes, and her lips were coated in pale pink sheen. The dress fit her perfectly.

"Oh, Livy, I've never seen a more beautiful woman."

"You look rather fantastic yourself. A tuxedo should be your required uniform." She smiled.

He chuckled. "Only if that dress is required. This party would be awful if you weren't here."

"Then I'm glad I came."

Gabe held out his arm for her. "Are you ready?"

A smile lit up her face, and she wrapped her hand around his bicep. "Yeah, I'm ready."

They walked down the hall and stopped at the stairs as voices filtered up from the first floor. "You aren't nervous, are you?" he asked.

She shook her head. "Um, a little, but only because I'm not used to parties."

"You think you could get used to them?"

She gave him a weak smile. "I don't know. I guess I'll see how this one goes."

He chuckled. "Good answer."

As they descended the stairs, Peter and Krista came into view. "Oh, you look fantastic, Livy," Krista said. "You actually make this guy look somewhat appealing."

"Hey. Not nice." Gabe chuckled.

Krista giggled and then pressed her hand on her stomach. "Oh, Ethan didn't like that."

Gabe smiled. "I love that kid already. He and I are going to be buds."

Krista smacked his arm. "You said that about Carolina and Jack."

"And Henry and Sam," Lauren added as she stopped next to Krista.

"Hey, I can't help it that I'm the favorite uncle."

Krista looked at Livy. "He's not lying, but only because he spoils them rotten."

Lauren nodded. "Oh, no kidding. I'm still hearing how Uncle Gabe took Sam to a tea party last summer and let her get her nails done. After taking her on a balloon ride."

Brenden and Millie stopped next to Lauren. "What are we talking about?"

"Gabe's innate ability to spoil our children."

Brendan glared at him a second. "Oh, that balloon ride? I'm never going to top that."

Millie reached through them and tugged on Gabe. "Love, we need to mingle."

"Okay," Livy said. She started to pull her arm free, and Gabe caught it. "What are you doing?"

"You need to mingle."

He put his arm around her waist and leaned down, whispering, "I asked you to this because I wanted you with me. That includes mingling."

When he straightened, she caught his gaze and held it. "I'd rather be with you anyway."

It was the best thing she could have said. Those words gave him hope that his feelings weren't one-sided. That she could see them together. Hopefully permanently.

Over the next hour as the guests continued to arrive, Gabe drifted through the house, introducing himself and Livy. She was more at ease than she gave herself credit for. She was articulate and witty, and people were drawn to her.

Once dinner was over, his mom gave him his cue to make the announcement. He stood and waited for everyone to quiet. "In case you don't know, I'm Gabriel Saxon, CEO of Saxon Publishing. Rumors have been circulating that we are purchasing Romero Publishing, and if this dinner party wasn't enough of a confirmation, then let me take away any doubt. We have purchased Romero. I want to take this opportunity to assure you that you won't be lost in the merger. I'm not saying there won't be changes, but you have my guarantee that those changes won't be done without serious consideration. At Saxon, we believe strongly in family, and once you are a member of our family, it means something." He paused and picked up his glass of champagne. "To a long and happy blended family."

Gabe took his seat again as everyone cheered and clinked glasses, and Livy closed her hand around his, leaning in. "You're amazing. You know that?"

It was business. He didn't think about it. "It was just a small announcement."

She held his gaze for a second. "It was more than that. Without so much as a clearing of the throat, you had this entire room's attention. You have this air of confidence and authority. Without even knowing you, you command respect. I don't know how you could have ever thought you needed to prove yourself. I'm in awe of you."

He pressed his lips to hers, resisting the urge to show her what she really meant to him. "I will keep that in mind for the future." And he'd do everything in his power to keep that awe too. He'd be a man she could respect and love.

When he lifted his head, Rachelle smiled at him from across the room. Livy followed his line of sight, and her lips pinched together. "I don't like her."

"Let me go show her the exit, okay?" With a small kiss, he stood and crossed the room.

Rachelle's arm was linked with a man he didn't know. "Rachelle."

"Oh, hello, Gabe. Nice party."

"This is a company party. Why are you here?"

The man shook Gabe's hand. "Jackson Kimball, agent with the Garnet Regency Lit Group."

"Nice to meet you. Gabriel Saxon. I take it you have authors with us?"

"Yes, four actually. Or, now four. Three were with Romero."

Gabe turned and saw Livy leave the room. She didn't look upset, so he returned his attention to Jackson. "Well, we're glad to have your authors with us."

"Jackson, I'm going to grab another glass of champagne. Should I get you one?" Rachelle asked.

"Yes. Thank you."

Rachelle gave Gabe a tight smile and pecked Jackson the cheek. "Be right back." He watched as she left, keeping an eye on where she was going.

"So, why did you want to purchase Romero?"

Gabe looked at Jackson. "What?"

"Why did Saxon purchase Romero?"

"There were a lot of reasons, but primarily to grow our company." He looked out over the crowd. Now both Livy and Rachelle were nowhere to be seen, and Gabe's stomach sank.

He didn't doubt Livy was strong, but Rachelle was cruel. She'd reduced some of the most confident women he knew to tears. What would she do to his Livy if she got her claws into her?

Turning to Jackson, he said, "If you'll excuse me, I need to mingle a little."

"Oh sure. Nice meeting you."

"You too," Gabe said and shook his hand before leaving in search of Livy.

CHAPTER 22

*L*ivy stepped inside the family room and let the quiet envelop her. The party wasn't bothering her, but she needed a moment to allow the hum of a hundred people to stop buzzing in her ears. She crossed her arm over her chest and palmed her forehead with her hand.

Gabe had been brilliant, and, man, did he look fantastic in that tuxedo. He was a beautiful man even in jeans, but tonight he'd made her mouth go dry. He'd commanded that room better than a musical conductor. Every eye had been on him, and all he had to do was stand up.

"Don't like the party?"

Livy whirled around.

Leaned against the frame of the door was Rachelle. "You do seem a little out of your element."

"Actually, it's a lovely party. I just needed a moment of quiet, which I've had, and now I'll return to it." She shocked herself with the response. It sounded poised and confident.

"You really think he cares about you, don't you?"

"I think he's a sweet man. Whether he cares for me or not is none of your concern."

The woman's eyebrows slowly rose. "He told me about you."

Livy's chest tightened. What could this woman possibly know about her? "I doubt that since we've been together the entire time we've been in New York."

"Really? The entire time? He never left your side?"

The color drained from Livy's face. He'd gone to get a tuxedo.

Rachelle's lips twitched into a wicked little smile. She pushed off the frame and walked into the room. "The poor orphan who attacked a sibling and spent the next ten years bouncing from home to home until she aged out. According to your version, you were the victim, but he didn't seem to believe that part of the story."

Her stomach lurched. Gabe wouldn't have. He'd

been good to her. Even if he no longer wanted her after the party was over, she'd never gotten the impression that he'd betray her. Surely Gabe wouldn't have told Rachelle, but how else would she have gotten the information?

"He's always loved being the guy to rush in and save the damsel in distress. I can't tell you the number of women Gabe has saved. It always ends with him getting a little thank you, if you know what I mean. Of course, they fall in love with him, but Gabe is mine. He always has been, and he always will be."

"How about you tell her where you really got that information, Rachelle?" Gabe stepped inside the room behind her.

Rachelle spun on her heels, and her eyes widened for a split second before she recovered her cool composure. "Oh, hey, Gabe. Livy and I were just talking. That's all."

"Right. Why don't you tell Livy exactly how you got that information since you didn't get it from me?"

She straightened her shoulders. "I did tell. You. When you went to get your tuxedo, you came to see me."

"Is that so? Are you sure it couldn't be that you used your father's password to get into his computer and then used his connections to get information about her? You do know that's a felony, right?"

Gabe brushed past Rachelle and stopped in front of Livy. "Her father is the Commissioner of the New York City Human Resources Department. She did a search of your name and went from there. Her father has a lot of powerful connections all over the country, and no doubt she used her father's name to get information on you."

He turned to Rachelle. "I don't know how to make it any clearer. We are done. You used government resources, and knowing how you operate, you lied to get information about her. This goes beyond just doing an internet search. You tampered with closed government files. I'll see to it that you get a six-by-nine for the maximum number of years if you ever come near me or Livy again."

Livy looked at Rachelle and watched the color drain from her face. There was no way Gabe was lying. Not with as pale as she was.

"Have I made myself clear?" he asked.

Rachelle nodded and quickly left the room.

Gabe tugged Livy into in arms and rubbed her back. "I'm so sorry. I should have known she'd find a way to attend."

"I didn't think you'd tell, but she knew things only you'd know."

He leaned back and took her face in his hands. "I know. I'm just glad I came looking for you and caught her in here with you."

"It was hard not to believe her."

"I told you, you're safe with me. All of you is safe with me."

She nodded. "I know...it's just..." Looking down, her heart spilled onto the floor. "It's just that when you said you wanted to talk after the party, I figured you were done with me, so—"

"Done with you? What are you talking about?"

"Anytime someone has wanted to talk to me, it was to tell me they were done with me. That they didn't want me anymore. I figured that's what you wanted to tell me." She quickly continued. "But I want you to know that this has been the best two weeks of my life. You've taught me so much, and your family is what I've always dreamed of. I'm so glad to have met you. You've changed how I see myself. I'm not saying there aren't insecurities hanging on, but you've given me the strength to see that I'm worth being loved. That I don't have to accept sloppy seconds."

Gabe stared at her, his lips parted like he didn't know how to respond.

"Being snowed in with you was the best thing to ever happen to me. I have a past, but I don't have to let that past rule my future. I can love and be loved. And it's because of the way you've treated me. It's the way your whole family has treated me."

GABE WAS SO DUMBSTRUCK he couldn't speak. She really thought he was going to tell her it was over? He was sure he'd given her no reason to think that. "Livy, I wanted to talk to you after the party because I wanted to make sure my focus was on you. I wanted to talk to you about our future. Where you saw this going."

She blinked. "What?" The question came out breathy.

He cupped her cheek. "I don't see a future where you're not in it. I'm not done with you. Not even close."

"You aren't?"

He shook his head. "No, sweetheart. I'm in love with you. I want all of you, all of the time, forever. I don't want you in my guest room anymore. I want to come home to you and see that hideous car you call transportation sitting in the driveway. I want to build a future with you."

"You love me?"

How could she not know that? Even without him saying it, he was pretty sure his actions had. "Every inch of me loves every inch of you. And since there are more inches of me than there are of you, I'm pretty sure that means double."

Slowly, a smile curved on her lips. Her big gray eyes locked with his. "I'm so used to not being wanted that it was an automatic thought. I don't fit in your world, so it never occurred to me that you'd want to me to stay."

"Well, I do, and you fit perfectly. Unless you don't want me."

"Of course I want you. I love you."

He smiled, and his heart pounded in his chest. "You love me?"

"Yes, with all my heart. You're the sweetest, kindest man I've never known. I've never felt safer in my life than when you hold me. I want to love you and be loved by you. And forever doesn't sound long enough."

Gabe continued to hold her gaze. "That's exactly what I thought too."

Livy stepped into him and palmed his chest with both

hands. "You helped me realize I didn't want mediocre anymore. I can't imagine loving anyone as much as I love you. I don't want to be loved by anyone but you because any love from anyone else would only ever be mediocre."

"Nothing I feel for you is even close to mundane. I've never been this happy. I have peace when I'm with you." He wrapped his arms around her waist and lifted her off the floor. "I want you. Always and forever."

He cupped the back of her head and gently brought her lips to his. "I want to wake up to you. I want to fall asleep next to you. I want everything to be with you. And the only thing that would make you more wonderful than you already are is for you to become Olivia Saxon."

She nodded. "I think we can make this merger work."

Gabe threw his head back and laughed. "I think so too."

Then he touched his lips to hers again, and there was nothing gentle about it. It spoke of promises for the future, long years ahead, holding hands, and cuddling in front of the fireplace. This kiss was hungry and insatiable.

He held her and kissed her, pouring all of himself into her, leaving no doubt that he belonged to her now and forever. There was nothing but her and his love for her.

When he pulled back, flushed and gasping for air, he touched his forehead to hers. "I suspect I need to return to the dinner party."

"I guess so."

"Would you dance with me?"

"Forever and always." She pressed a soft kiss to his lips. "All of me and all of my dances belong to you."

EPILOGUE

Ten months later...

"Oh, honey, you just look stunning."

Livy grinned. "You think so?"

With a kiss on the cheek, Millie embraced her. "I sure do. Gabe is going to be beside himself."

The door to the church's dressing room opened. Tori, Kath, Lauren, and Krista walked in. "Oh, wow. Livy, that dress really was the one," Tori said.

Livy turned and looked in the mirror. She'd picked it because she loved it and she knew Gabe would love seeing her in it. It hit her curves in just the right places, and from experience, she'd learned that he loved it when she wore things that accentuated them.

Krista stepped forward and held out a box.

"What's this?" asked Livy as she lifted the box from Krista's hand.

She looked from Livy to the other four women in the room. "We decided we wanted to take care of your something borrowed, something blue, something old, and something new."

"This is something borrowed," Krista said.

Livy opened it and giggled. "The earrings Peter got you." She'd mentioned to Krista that she loved them.

"What better day to borrow them?"

Lauren gave Livy her gift, and she opened it; a blue garter belt. "Something blue."

Lauren chuckled. "Maybe not the cleverest thing, but I'm sure Gabe will love it."

Tori went next. When Livy got the box open, her mouth dropped open. "Oh, Tori, this is beautiful." The hair comb was delicate with a row of sparkling diamonds and a little ruby butterfly.

"It's old, but appropriate. You've broken out of your shell the last ten months and have shown the world what I've known. That Olivia Weber is someone worth knowing and loving."

"You're going to make me ruin my makeup," Livy said as she touched her fingers to the edges of her eyes.

"And this is from me," Kath said, and Millie cleared her throat. "Okay, so it's from me and Mom."

Livy nodded as she opened the gift. Inside was a bracelet with the words engraved: *always family*. She lifted her gaze and let it sweep from Kath to Millie. "Thank you."

"You were always one of us. Today is only making it official, sis," Kath said.

Tears pricked Livy's eyes as she pulled the bracelet out, and Millie put it on for her.

"Always family, honey. Always," Millie said as tears pooled in her eyes as well. "We love you, Livy."

The women gathered around her and hugged her. They'd impacted her life more than they'd ever know. Their strength, character, confidence, and love had given her something she never would have dreamed of: the ability to release the past, see the future, and embrace the love of the people around her.

Family didn't have to be related. They just had to be loving, and that's what she'd found with Gabe Saxon.

A knock on the door drew their attention as it cracked open. The wedding planner peeked in. "It's time. Are you ready?"

"More than ready."

They walked to the sanctuary and stood at the

closed doors. One by one, her bridesmaids went through the door until it was just her and Millie.

Millie hooked her arm in Livy's. "Thank you for letting me give you away."

"I love you to pieces, Millie."

Gabe's mom patted her hand. "I love you to pieces too. I especially love how you love Gabe. You don't know how happy I am that he's marrying you."

The wedding processional started, and the doors opened as their friends and family stood. Everything fell away, and all Livy saw was Gabe standing at the front, waiting for her. Her heart had never been so full of joy. He was the man she'd been writing about, waiting for, and wanting.

It was all she could do not to run down the aisle and scream, "I do!" She'd dreamed of this moment for so long, and it was everything she wanted it to be. She loved telling the world how much she loved Gabe and knew forever wouldn't be nearly long enough to show him how much she loved him.

ABOUT THE AUTHOR

Bree Livingston lives in the West Texas Panhandle with her husband, children, and cats. She'd have a dog, but they took a vote and the cats won. Not in numbers, but attitude. They wouldn't even debate. They just leveled their little beady eyes at her and that was all it took for her to nix getting a dog. Her hobbies include...nothing because she writes all the time.

She loves carbs, but the love ends there. No, that's not true. The love usually winds up on her hips which is why she loves writing romance. The love in the pages of her books are sweet and clean, and they definitely don't add pounds when you step on the scale. Unless of course, you're actually holding a Kindle while you're weighing. Put the Kindle down and try again. Also, the cookie because that could be the problem too. She knows from experience.

Join her mailing list to be the first to find out publishing news, contests, and more by going to her website at https://www.breelivingston.com.

facebook.com/BreeLivingstonWrites

twitter.com/BreeLivWrites

bookbub.com/authors/bree-livingston